The black bra held her breasts tightly. As Diana reached behind her back to the zip of her skirt, her fleshy mounds were pushed out against the flimsy lace, trembling slightly. She could see his eyes on the dark tunnel of her cleavage.

She let the skirt fall to the floor. She stepped out of it slowly, raising one foot at a time. His eyes dropped to her legs.

'I didn't think anyone wore stockings any more,' he said.

'I do.'

As she reached behind her back to unhook the bra, he said, 'No.' His rich voice was full of authority. 'Let me . . .'

Amateur Days

Becky Bell

First published in 1994
by HEADLINE BOOK PUBLISHING

A HEADLINE DELTA paperback

10 9 8 7 6 5 4 3 2

ISBN 0 7472 4304 2

Phototypeset by Intype Ltd, London

Printed and bound in Great Britain by
Cox & Wyman Ltd, Reading, Berkshire

HEADLINE BOOK PUBLISHING
A division of Hodder Headline PLC
338 Euston Road
London NW1 3BH

Amateur Days

Chapter One

The timid knock on the bedroom door did not wake her. Diana Wilson was already awake.

'Come,' she said imperiously.

Her husband, Charles, shuffled into the bedroom carrying a breakfast tray. On the tray was the newspaper, a pot of coffee, a glass of freshly squeezed orange juice and two slices of wholemeal toast. Charles had not forgotten a neatly pressed white linen napkin either.

Diana sat up in bed. These days she slept naked. She did not bother to cover her breasts as she propped herself up against the pillows and Charles set the little wicker supports of the tray on either side of her lap. Her breasts were large but firm, their generous curves miraculously defying gravity as they tilted upward from her chest. Her nipples were big too, and for some reason were erect, the tender flesh corrugated and hard. Surrounding them her areolae were circles of a dark musty brown.

Relieved of the tray, Charles stood in his pyjamas and Paisley dressing gown looking at his feet, knowing better than to leave the room without permission. He could not stop himself from trying to sneak surreptitious glances at his wife's naked flesh.

'Go and get ready for work. Come back in fifteen minutes,' Diana ordered, her expression of contempt set in stone.

As soon as he had turned his back to leave, her face cracked; she could not help herself from breaking into a huge grin. Two months ago her life had changed. Totally. From being an obedient and faithful wife, prepared to put up with her husband's drinking and total lack of interest in her, she had become, so it seemed, a person in her own right, a woman with her own needs and, more essentially, the means to satisfy them.

It was all about sex. Ultimately it had been her dire sexual frustration that had catapulted her into her present position. If her husband had been at all interested in sex with her she would have not been tempted to accept the proposition of a stranger, albeit a handsome and attractive stranger, who had mistaken her for an escort in a hotel bar. But he hadn't and the frustration of being ignored sexually for years had lead her to the stranger's room. And that had been the beginning.

Over the next weeks she had been to lots of stranger's rooms. She had discovered her own vibrant sexuality. Like a volcano lain dormant for years, it had exploded, overwhelming her with feelings and sensations she would not have believed possible. Her body had become a well of untold pleasure. Sex took her over, invigorated her, vitalised her, made her realise what she had been missing all those years, made her a new woman.

Not wanting the experience to end she had enrolled in an escort service. Her first encounter had been accidental. But she didn't want to have to rely on chance. It was too important. By chance, however, it was through her enrolment that she had discovered the reason for her husband's lack of interest in having sex with her. Asked to help out Domina, one of the escort services more esoteric girls, with a client, she was astonished to find her husband was that client and even more surprised at the services he required. Naked, gagged, blind-folded and chained to a punishment frame her husband had been whipped, abused and humiliated while she looked on. Her husband wanted to be a slave and Domina had been his regular mistress.

At first Diana had been horrified and returned home determined on divorce. But her mood had changed. If her husband wanted to be a slave then he could be her slave, at least until it suited her. Considering all the money he'd spent and all the lies he'd told to visit Domina so frequently, she would be quite happy to treat him like dirt. And if she got bored with taking her anger out on him she could always throw him out. With what she knew about him there would be no trouble over the divorce. Meanwhile, for as long as it amused her, she had decided she would let him serve her in the way he seemed so keen to do . . .

Diana drank the orange juice and poured herself a cup of coffee. Tonight was Carolyn's party and she was going to spend the day looking for a house. It was going to be a busy day.

She had decided to buy a new house. She wanted something bigger, something in the country just outside London, not in the suburbs, something old and pretty, something that did not remind her of her marriage and her previous life. With what she was earning now, she could afford it.

Not that she was doing it for the money. The money was a bonus, the icing on the cake. If she was honest with herself, really honest, she would have to say she would do it for nothing. The excitement she felt, even with the most unprepossessing client, had not diminished. She still got hot and sticky with anticipation. She had tried to analyse it and had reached the conclusion it was something to do with the fact that when she met a man it was for one reason only: sex. No skirting around the subject, no will-I-won't-I. They were both there for sex, plain and simple. Somehow it was the directness of it that made it exciting. The money was incidental, welcome but irrelevant.

Only eating one slice of toast she read *The Times* until fifteen minutes later, exactly, there was another timid knock on the bedroom door.

'Come,' she said, resuming her cold ungiving tone.

Charles advanced into the room, wearing his business suit. It fitted him a great deal better than it had. Charles' extensive paunch was beginning to recede. Diana had put him on a strict diet and his consummation of beer had been completely curtailed. She had put him on a strict exercise routine too. In fact everything about Charles' life was strict at the moment.

'I've finished,' Diana told him.

Without a word, Charles took the tray from her lap.

'Come straight back,' she said as he took the tray downstairs. She pulled back the bedclothes and got out of bed.

By the time she had showered Charles was back, standing uneasily by the door, looking at his feet. Patting herself dry with a large white bath towel, Diana came back into the bedroom from the en suite bathroom and clucked in annoyance.

'Didn't you knock?' she said. 'I didn't tell you to come in.'

'I thought . . .' he mumbled still looking down at his feet.

'When are you going to learn Charles? I do your thinking for you.'

Satisfied she was dry Diana dropped the towel and stood in front of the long mirror on the wardrobe door. She was pleased with what she saw. Her tall body was firm and ripe, her skin a glowing fresh pink, her long almost-blonde hair shining and clean. She was the picture of health. Though her breasts were large and heavy, the rest of her body was slim, her navel iron-flat, her waist waspie and pinched, her legs fine and contoured with well-defined hollows in her thighs under the shadow of her pubic triangle. She turned round and looked over her shoulder so she could admire the rich curves of her buttocks. Her arse was high and tight, its central cleft deep and dark. She turned again and watched herself as she ran her hand into her thick fair pubic hair, fluffed up by the towel. She stroked it gently. The hair was so thick it completely hid the crease of her sex.

Ignoring Charles completely, she walked over to the chest of drawers where she kept her underwear.

She had bought a lot of new lingerie in recent
weeks. She intended to buy a lot more. Before what
she had come to think of as The Event, her encounter in the hotel bar, she had thought little about
what underwear she wore. Cotton knickers and
practical bras. Now she luxuriated in silks and
Lycra, satin and lace. Before, she hadn't even
owned a suspender belt. Now she had basques and
teddies and suspender belts and G-strings all in
matching colours: dark blues, flame reds, exotic
purples, not to mention black.

Rifling through the drawers she found a set in
black silk and lace – a deep-cut bra, French knickers, suspender belt. From another drawer she took
a packet of gun-metal grey stockings.

She knew Charles was watching her every movement though trying to pretend he wasn't. Where
once he had not had the slightest desire to look at
her, naked or dressed, now he would drool over her.
He knew he was not allowed to touch. He knew
this display was deliberate, part of his punishment,
a tease, part of her control over him.

Diana slipped into her bra and reached behind
her back to clip it into place. It pushed her breasts
together slightly to form a deep cleavage. She
pulled the suspender belt around her waist and
clipped that on too, its long black suspenders hanging down over her thighs like strange, alien
fingers.

She held the French knickers out in front of her,
pulling the waistband open before she bent to put
her feet in them. She made sure she bent with her
back to Charles so he would see the whole of her
sex, fringed with thick pubic hair, but exposed, a

long slit of labia, fleshy, thick labia, and the puckered corona of her anus, like an inverted barnacle. Slowly, she straightened up again, pulling the lacy silk over her finely contoured thighs, up over the curves of her buttocks until the waistband fitted neatly over the waist of the suspender belt and the secrets of her sex were veiled by soft black silk.

Charles' erection jutted from the front of his trousers. It would get no relief.

Diana sat on the edge of the bed. She undid the cellophane packet and extracted the stockings, letting the packaging drop to the floor by her feet.

'Pick it up,' she ordered.

Charles stooped forward immediately, reaching for the cellophane, his head inches from her knees, his erection nudging into his navel. As he stood up he eyed the triangle of her lap where the black silk struggled to contain her thick pubic hair.

She rolled one of the stockings into a neat pocket around the reinforced toe and extended her leg. She pointed her toe and pulled the pocket of nylon on to her foot. Slowly she played the nylon out over her calf, up over her thigh. Her toe pointed directly at her husband's tumescence. His eyes watched every movement. The crotch of the French knickers wasn't tight like some of the panties she wore. With her leg raised he could glimpse, no more than a tantalising glimpse, the lips of her sex.

He gave up any pretence that he was staring at the floor. He watched as the grey nylon, woven with Lycra to give it a slippery sheen, encased her thighs. He watched as her long elegant fingers took the tongue of metal at the end of the suspender and slipped it between her creamy flesh and the

nylon, then pressed the little rubber circle down
into it catching the darker grey welt of the stocking
and pulling it into a taut peak. The rubber was
covered with a little sash of black satin cut on a
diagonal like the blade of a scalpel.

Diana repeated the process with the other leg.
She wanted him to remember how she had looked:
he would carry the image with him all day. She
pulled the second stocking over her leg, smoothed
the nylon completely flat then clipped in the suspenders at the front and side of her thigh. She
stood up and smoothed the nylon again, running
the palms of both her hands up the shiny material,
making sure it was not wrinkled.

From the wardrobe she selected a white blouse
and a black suit. Very businesslike. With her back
to Charles she slipped into a pair of heels, high
heels but by no means her highest. Charles would
be looking at the way the French knickers just
revealed the crescents of her buttocks where they
met the top of her thighs.

'You'd better go,' she said sitting at her dressing
table and beginning to pin her long hair up. 'I don't
want you to be late.'

'Oh . . .' he whimpered pathetically.

She swivelled around on the dressing table stool.

'Oh what, Charles?' She looked at him sternly,
her expression brooking no disagreement.

'Nothing,' he said turning to go.

'I'm going to a party tonight with Ann. Make
sure you're home on time. I want the house cleaned
up before she gets here.'

'I'll be on time,' he said.

'Go,' she ordered. She watched him leave in the

dressing table mirror, then concentrated on her hair.

He would be on time. From having been late practically every night – either out drinking with his cronies or tied to Domina's punishment frame – Charles had got home on the dot every night. Of course, Diana had made it perfectly clear to him what would happen if he was not. He would be out, out of the house and out of her life. She had also made it clear that at the moment his situation was only temporary. She might decide to throw him out anyway. When she found a new house there might be room for him and there might not. It all depended on how well he behaved. So far his behaviour had been impeccable. He had obeyed her to the letter. For Charles, of course, the rod of iron with which he was now ruled was paradise come true. The only question was how long Diana condescended to play her part.

It certainly had its advantages. He would do anything. Clean the house, shop, wash the clothes. Anything he was ordered to do.

She heard the front door slam and the crunch of feet on the gravel drive. Naturally he had to take the train to work these days. Glancing at her watch she hurried with her make-up then left the bedroom just as it was. Charles would clear it up later.

Downstairs she found the car keys and the map of Buckinghamshire she had bought. It would take her forty minutes, she estimated, to drive to her first appointment.

By three o'clock in the afternoon Diana Wilson was

thoroughly depressed. She had seen four houses
and they were all different shades of terrible – too
run-down, too cramped, too damp, or just too plain
awful. All had looked wonderful in the estate
agent's photographs taken from a cunning angle
that neatly hid their worst feature, on a sunny day.

There was only one more to see, equally attractive from the glossy colour photograph but, she
feared, probably destined to be equally
disappointing.

The estate agent was young and appeared nervous in her presence. He talked too much and, after
the second visit, she had decided to follow him in
her car rather than letting him drive her. So, now,
she followed his Ford Sierra down a winding
country lane and through a pillared gateway cut in
a tall thick beech hedge and into the circular driveway of a Georgian manor house, its neat portico
flanked by two bay trees topiared into perfect
spheres and sitting in large terracotta pots.

Getting out of her car she suppressed her
excitement. Though, for once, the picture in her
hand matched the exterior view, no doubt there
was something untoward hidden away behind the
façade that would dissolve her initial impression.
There had to be something. A pig farm at the back,
a dank dark interior with raging woodworm, terminal dry rot, something.

The estate agent rang the doorbell talking con-
stantly. 'It's beautiful isn't it? Georgian. Grade Two
listed. Only been on the market a week. The
owner's got to go abroad apparently. Five bedrooms,
three bathrooms, three large receptions. And
there's a full cellar. Very secluded as you can
see . . .'

The door opened.

'Hello,' the man standing in the doorway said, 'please come in. It's starting to get a bit colder now, isn't it?' His voice was deep and rich, the vocal equivalent of velvet. It matched his appearance perfectly. He was tall, with a strong square-jawed face, greying hair and the palest ice-blue eyes Diana had ever seen. Though he was probably in his fifties, his body looked strong and well-exercised; a thick thatch of chest hair protruded from his open shirt at the throat, his waist line betraying not an inch of fat. He wore only a pair of corduroy slacks and the blue cotton shirt.

'Mr Borland, this is Ms Wilson,' the estate agent said, emphasising the 'Ms' as his boss had told him to do, after seeing a television programme that had proved conclusively that women reacted better if not addressed as 'Miss' or 'Mrs', and were more liable to purchase whatever they were viewing — clothes, cars, houses.

'How do you do?' Borland said, stepping aside to let them into the hall then extending his hand to Diana.

Diana shook it firmly. Their eyes met across their hands. Diana felt as though she had been hit by lightning, a shock that seemed to invade her most intimate feelings.

'Hello,' was all she could manage to say.

'Well, why don't you help yourselves,' he said indicating the house. 'I'll be down here if you have any questions. Please feel free.'

'Thanks,' the estate agent said. 'We'll start upstairs shall we?'

Diana wasn't listening. She was watching Borland walk back into his living room.

11

They toured the house and the gardens. Diana found it hard to concentrate. Borland's eyes haunted her. There was something about the expression on his face, something knowing, as if he could read her secrets, knew all her secrets. She felt her pulse racing. He was so attractive, so smooth, so at ease with himself, his power, physical and mental, only too obvious.

She tried to put it out of her mind, but could not help looking for evidence of a woman in the house. There was none.

They left the living room till last. Borland sat reading in front of a big log fire, his legs crossed, both hands holding the book. Outside the room, a large lawn was speckled with the first leaves of autumn from the many surrounding trees. The view was impressive, rolling countryside spread out over a gently undulating valley. There was no pig farm.

'I can't claim credit for the garden, I'm afraid,' Borland said, putting a bookmark in the pages and getting up. 'I've got a marvellous gardener. Don't worry he's included in the purchase price.' He smiled. His teeth were white and regular. He was looking at her again. She could feel his eyes examining every inch of her body. She had this strange feeling that he could see right through her clothes. Then his eyes met hers. They bored into her, as though looking for her soul.

'It's a beautiful house,' Diana said, not wanting to talk about the house at all.

'Great . . . great. I knew you'd love it.' The estate agent said, his whole body restless with movement in comparison to Borland's still poise. 'Well we've

just got time to get over to Westlands...' he said,
looking at his watch.

'Can I offer you something before you go?' Borland said. His eyes had not left hers for a second.
If he had blinked she must have missed it and she
didn't think she had.

'No,' the estate agent answered, 'it's very nice of
you but we've got to go...'

'You go,' Diana said.

'We're expected at four...'

'Make my apologies...'

'Sorry?'

'I want to have another look around here. Make
my apologies. I'll see it another day.'

'Oh,' the estate agent looked non-plussed.

'Do you want to use my phone?' Borland asked.

'Yes, yes. Would you mind?'

'Over there,' Borland said indicating a small table
by the door. As the estate agent got his office to
cancel the next appointment, Borland went over
to a large Victorian secretaire. It had been con-
verted into a drinks cabinet, the bottom half con-
taining a fridge. From this he took out a bottle of
Louis Roederer Crystal and two champagne flutes.
He opened the bottle effortlessly, with no popping
cork or uncontrolled flow of wine.

'All done,' the estate agent reported. 'So where
shall we start? Upstairs again? Or the gardens?'

'You can go now,' Diana said.

'Sorry?'

'Go,' Diana repeated bluntly.

'Oh... I...' The estate agent didn't know
whether he should leave a beautiful client alone in
a strange house with a strange man. Where did his

13

duty lie? His boss hadn't covered this eventuality.

'I'll show Ms Wilson around,' Borland said helpfully.

The estate agent hesitated. He was blushing slightly. 'Well ... I suppose ... If you're sure?'

'Positive,' Diana said and meant it.

'O.K. You'll call me then?'

'In the morning.'

'Great. Bye then.' He hesitated again before walking out with obvious reluctance.

'Alone at last,' said Diana pointedly.

Borland handed her the glass of champagne. 'It's probably against their code of ethics ...'

'What ethics?'

'Estate agents code of practice.'

'That's rules not ethics.'

'Very precise.' He said it with no hint of mockery.

'If it's against the rules it must be fun. Cheers.'

'Cheers,' he said. They clinked glasses and sipped at the cool wine.

'Do you want to fuck me here or upstairs?' Diana said calmly with no hint of emotion. It was not a matter of emotion. She knew what she wanted. She knew what he wanted. It was in his eyes. What was the point in pretending, in sitting making small talk for an hour before they got to it? This was the new Diana Wilson. The experience of the last months had freed her, made her take control of her life, take what she wanted.

'That's refreshingly direct,' he said.

'And?'

By way of reply he put the champagne glass down on an occasional table, went to a huge wicker basket of logs, threw six or seven into the vast

14

grate and came back to stand in front of her. He put both hands up to her face, cupping her cheeks and drawing her forward until their lips were just touching. Instead of kissing her he moved his head from side to side so his lips brushed against hers. Only after long seconds of this did his grip tighten to hold her face firmly as he pressed his mouth down on to hers and plunged his tongue into her.

She felt his hands moulding her cheeks, as though trying to shape her mouth, make it tight around his tongue. She sucked on it then licked it with her own. It was thick and hot.

His hands left her face and his arms snaked around her back, hugging her body into his and kissing her harder still. She wrapped her arms around his broad back and felt his body against her. It was muscled and strong. Her head was tipped back by his height; he was leaning over her, their faces almost horizontal. She could feel his erection growing rapidly but no faster than her own excitement. Her body was alive with sensation but it was her mind that was driving the engine of her passion, it was her mind telling her how exciting it was to be here with a total stranger, abandoning herself, giving herself, wild, wanton, open.

She broke the kiss needing air. They parted slightly and their eyes met again.

'You've made me very hard,' he said, as though merely stating a fact.

Diana looked down at his trousers. Immediately she ran her hand over the bulge then gripped it tight. She could feel its heat through the material. She squeezed it.

'So I have,' she said coquettishly. 'What do you

suppose I should do with it now?'

Without waiting for an answer she dropped to her knees in front of him and found the metal tongue of his zip. Pulling it down she fished inside. He was wearing striped boxer shorts. She parted their open fly and found what she was looking for. His cock, like his tongue, was thick and hot. She pulled it out into the open. It was already wet, the circumcised tip glistening in the firelight. It was a handsome cock she thought, the glans as smooth and polished as a pebble on a beach and shaped like the helmet of some futuristic space invader.

With the very tip of her tongue she probed the little slit of his urethra. His cock reacted immediately, pulsing in her hand. She pushed her tongue down into the slit and felt him pulse again. Then she opened her mouth and lunged forward sucking his cock in, taking it down as deep into her throat as it would go. He moaned. Diana's body reacted too. She felt a damp warmth spreading between her legs. She thought she could feel her clitoris swelling like a cock in miniature.

His hands found the back of her head, at first just caressing her fair hair, then pulling out the pins that held it up. Soon her long hair was free. He combed it with his fingers, fanning it out then letting it drop back on to her shoulders.

'Beautiful,' he said. She was not sure whether he meant her hair or what she was doing to his cock.

Her hand worked its way into his flies and found his balls. Try as she might she could not extract them from the folds of material, so, with both hands and without taking his cock from her mouth, she undid his belt and the waist button of the slacks and pulled them and the boxer shorts down over his legs. The trousers fell to his ankles but the shorts hung on his cock as it was protruding through their fly. Quickly, she drew her mouth away, freed the shorts from the obstacle and then plunged her mouth back down on the hard solid stem which now glistened with her saliva. She tried to get it all the way in, right down into her throat. Her hands slid round his hips to his buttocks, taking one cheek in each. She dug her fingers into them like claws. His flesh was hard with muscle. The feel of his strong arse excited her.

She began a rhythm using her hands to push him forward into her mouth, then withdrawing until the rim of his glans was at her lips, then plunging his whole cock deep again until his curly pubic hair tickled her chin. Long wet strokes, making her mouth cling to his cock, her tongue pressed against its underside. Diana felt her whole body tingling with excitement. She wouldn't have minded if he spunked. But he pulled away.

'I thought I was going to fuck you,' he said.

'Didn't you like what I was doing?'

'Yes, but it's very one-sided. I like sex for two.'

He pulled off his shoes and socks without sitting down and disentangled his trousers and boxer shorts from his ankles. Diana got to her feet a little unsteadily. His shirt was discarded revealing the thick hair of his chest. It was curly, pointing in no particular direction. The hair on his navel was finer, more silky, all the hairs forming a long V pointing like an arrow to his cock. The hair at the top of his chest, like the hair on his head, had turned grey.

His cock stuck out from his body like a rod of

17

steel. He had no embarrassment about his nakedness. He had no reason to. It looked as good as it felt. His limbs were contoured with muscle, his chest deep, his arms broad, his navel flat.

Diana realised she was staring.

In front of the fire, now burning briskly with the new logs, was a thick cream wool rug. He took up his glass of champagne, took a sip, then lay down on his side on the rug, the champagne still in his hand, his cock showing no signs of diminishing.

'Do you want me to undress you?' he asked.

'No,' she said. 'I'd like you to watch me.'

'I think that would be very exciting.'

Diana was perfectly cool. Though her excitement was coursing through her body like an express train, though she could feel her sex throbbing between her legs like some hungry animal, she was still in control. She stripped off her suit jacket and threw it on an armchair. Unbuttoning the white blouse she pulled it from the waistband of the skirt and shucked herself out of it. It joined her jacket on the chair.

Three months ago, God knows what underwear she would have been wearing. She was delighted her attitude had changed. Borland was clearly delighted too. She could see the effect the black silk and lace were having on him. His eyes had narrowed, his cock was producing a tear of fluid.

The black bra held her large breasts tightly. As she reached behind her back to the zip of her skirt, her breasts were pushed out against the black lace, trembling slightly. She could see his eyes on the dark tunnel of her cleavage. Was he imagining what it would be like to nestle his cock there? The thought made her shiver with pleasure.

She let the skirt fall to the floor. She stepped out of it slowly, raising one foot at a time. His eyes dropped to her legs.

'I didn't think anyone wore stockings any more,' he said quietly.

'I do.'

She stooped to pick up the skirt from the floor and threw it onto the chair with her other clothes. As she reached behind her back to unhook the bra he said, 'No.' His rich voice was full of authority. 'Let me,' he said more softly.

Without a word she knelt on the rug, turning her back to him so he could reach the fastening of the bra. As his fingers reached the hooks his lips kissed her spine. The strap of the bra parted but instead of letting it fall free, he gathered the two ends in his hands and pulled them together again, tighter, tighter than they had been before. Her breasts were squeezed together. Then he released the strap and moved his hands around under the black silk, under her arms, until his fingers were under the now loose cups as his palms cupped her breasts instead. He kissed her neck, all over her neck as far as his mouth could reach, making a ring of kisses, a necklace of kisses.

Diana felt herself swooning, melting, her whole body turning liquid. His mouth was hot and wet.

His fingers had found her nipples. It was not difficult. They were as hard as rubies and as red. With the bra still hanging from her shoulders, he took the knots of flesh between the thumb and forefinger of both hands and pinched.

'Ah ...' Diana exclaimed, but not from pain.

Immediately, he pulled her round to face him. He cupped her face in his hands again and kissed her full on the mouth, at the same time pushing her over on to her side. She rolled over and straightened her legs. Without breaking his hold on her face or the kiss he slid on top of her. She felt his penis, hard as a rock, against the silk of her knickers.

Releasing her cheeks from his hands and her lips from his mouth he pulled the bra away from her breasts. They quivered at their freedom. His eyes looked into hers unwaveringly as his hand weighed both breasts in turn before descending smoothly down to the waistband of her French knickers. He eased their bodies apart and pulled the knickers down. She co-operated, raising her buttocks off the rug. When his hand had dragged the knickers down to her ankles she kicked them away.

His eyes left her face to look down at her near-naked body. She could see them examining her breasts, her navel, the thick tuft of her pubic hair, her long thighs bisected by the welt of the grey stockings. He made no attempt to take her stockings off.

Then his eyes locked on to hers again. They seemed to be searching there for some meaning, some reason, as though he wanted to know why she had suddenly given herself to him so easily. His hand ran over her navel, the tips of his fingers disappearing into her thick pubic hair. In a second the tip of his finger was on her clitoris. It was wet, soaking wet. She parted her legs bending one knee. His finger ran the whole length of her labia, right down between her legs. Her labia felt puffy and swollen. Her cunt was completely liquid.

Back on her clitoris the tip of his finger pressed down on to the tiny bud of nerves, pressing it against her pubic bone before he started wanking it, moving it from side to side, using her wetness to make the motion effortless, frictionless.

Diana could not keep her eyes open any longer. What he was doing was so perfect, as though he had read in her eyes the secrets of her body.

'Don't stop . . .' she begged, wanting to make sure he understood the signals that her body was giving him, anxious that the delicious feeling shouldn't end.

'I won't,' he whispered.

His finger moved precisely, exactly, moving her clitoris to and fro like a metronome. She gasped. It was so good. She was coming. He was making her come. Lying on the floor, with a perfect stranger wanking her with such intimacy, it was as though he had known her for years. Her whole body tensed, every nerve wanting release. He sensed how near she was – like he'd sensed how to give her such exquisite pleasure – and dipped his head to sink his teeth into the tender puckered flesh of her nipple. Instead of just pinching it, he held it between his teeth and pulled his head back, pulling her breast up by the nipple, stretching it taut, making a pyramid. Then, at exactly the right moment for her, as she felt the first wave of her orgasm breaking over his finger, he released her nipple from his teeth. As her breast fell back she came, her whole body trembling as much as her breast, sensation locking every nerve in every muscle.

But he knew that was only the beginning. He waited just long enough for the orgasm to die in her, to run its course, and then, suddenly, miraculously it seemed to her as it happened so smoothly, his cock was jammed in her cunt to the hilt and he was on top of her. She couldn't remember him moving or thrusting: he was just there.

She had never felt a cock so hot. It burnt her like a hot poker. Her cunt clung to it, the contractions of her orgasm instantly renewed. He did not move. He just held it in her, arching his body so it was as deep as it would go, so the stem of his cock was pressed against her clitoris. He didn't need to move. Her body was shuddering under him. Whether this was another orgasm or the same one rekindled on the fire of his cock she did not know or care. But she felt herself plunging down into the dark throbbing abyss where all she could feel was the hardness of his cock and its heat and her own cunt melting over it. This time she heard herself screaming as her passion swamped everything else in her mind.

'Oh my God ...' she said. Her voice sounded strange as though it did not belong to her. She had lost track of time. How long had he been buried inside her? She opened her eyes with an effort but it was one she could not sustain. Her body wanted its darkness to wallow in the sensations it was still feeling.

His cock was moving now, sliding up and down her greased, slippery channel. She had wrapped her arms around his body. Now she slipped them down to his buttocks. She was in control of herself again. She wanted to make him come. She wanted to make him spunk inside her. She raised her legs, moving her thighs up so the angle of their bodies changed, his cock burrowing deep, finding another niche in her willing sex. She reached up with her mouth to kiss him. Their tongues vied for position. In the end she thrust her tongue into him.

But none of this gave him pause. His cock moved relentlessly. Up and down. Long slow strokes. But they were getting faster. Faster and faster as his control slipped, as his body made its demands. Faster and faster until he was ramming into her faster than she would have believed possible, a blur of movement, each stroke meeting the neck of her womb as her clitoris was pounded by the base of his cock. She could feel the muscles of his buttocks under her hands driving him forward.

He pulled his mouth away from hers, stopping the frantic movement.

'Do you want me to come?' he said, his voice thick with passion.

'Yes, yes ... come ...' she murmured, urging him forward by digging her fingers into his buttocks.

He straightened his arms and raised himself over her body so they were joined only at her hips, her stockinged thighs framing his pelvis. She looked down between their bodies. She could see his cock driving in and out of her. It glistened with her juices. Suddenly she felt her body spasm. The vision of his cock impaling itself in her was too much. Her cunt contracted again, clinging to the hot wet flesh of his cock as her body demanded another completion. Her eyes rolled back. Though she could not keep them open she could still see, in the blackness, his cock plunging down into her forest of pubic hair.

'Oh . . . oh . . . oh . . .' she gasped, unable to stop herself.

He felt her come. Felt her whole body squeeze itself on his cock, centred, focused on his spunk-filled, pulsing fire-hot cock.

Then it was his turn. He sank back down on her – flesh on flesh – feeling her stone-hard nipples on his chest. He was released now, free of everything but his own need he hammered into her again, hammered hard and fast, like a steam hammer, wanting to drive deeper and deeper, bury himself, intern himself in the wonderful liquid centre of his beautiful woman.

She could feel his spunk. She could feel his cock swelling as his spunk pumped it up. She felt him stop, stop deep inside her. He stopped everything, every movement and waited knowing he had found his place, waiting for his cock to spasm and take him over the edge.

Diana felt it buck inside her as it spat out his spunk. It seemed to go on for ever. Spasm after spasm, his cock jerking against the walls of her sex. Suddenly he plunged back and forth again, perhaps to get the last glimmer of sensation. Then he stopped and his whole body shook involuntarily like a dog shaking off water. Another moment's stillness and he shook again. Finally he was quiet.

Diana felt the heat of the fire on her side. She looked into the flames burning the big logs in the grate. His cock slipped out of her and he rolled off on to his side his arm resting across her navel.

'It seemed we both needed that,' he said.

'Yes.'

'So, Ms Wilson.' He emphasised 'Ms'.

'So, Mr Borland.' She emphasised 'Mr'.

'Exactly, I don't even know your first name.'

'Diana.'

'John. You're a remarkable lady, Diana.'

'And you're a remarkable man.'

'I'm glad you think so.'

He got up, found the champagne bottle and her discarded glass and brought them back to the fireside. Sitting crossed-legged on the rug he poured her a glass of champagne and refilled his own glass which was on the hearth where he'd left it. They clinked their glasses together before they sipped at the wine.

'I wish I'd made a condition beforehand,' he said.

'What sort of condition?'

'That you have dinner with me.'

She laughed. 'You mean so that I just don't want you for your body? Isn't that my line?'

'Will you?' he persisted.

'Yes. I'll give you my number. On one condition . . .'

'What condition?'

'That you fuck me again afterwards.'

It was his turn to laugh. 'Agreed. Definitely agreed.'

'And there's one other thing . . .'

'Yes . . .'

'I want to buy your house.'

Chapter Two

Diana drove the car more slowly than usual, aware that her concentration was likely to lapse. Her body was still humming, like a piano long after the notes had been struck, the vibrations of her multiple orgasms still tingling in her nerves. But, of course, there was the house to think about too. It was simply perfect. Exactly what she wanted, the right size and secluded, with no neighbours.

As she drove, she pictured what she would do with the rooms and which of the bedrooms she would have for herself. She was glad the garden came with a gardener: it was too big for her to cope with alone. In the morning she'd make an offer through the estate agent. She didn't want to complicate her relationship with Borland by calling him direct.

It was seven thirty by the time she got home. As she parked the car in the drive she noted with satisfaction that Charles was already home. The lights were on in his bedroom. Since her discovery of his sexual proclivities she had made him strip out all the carpet and furniture from the smallest of the spare rooms. He slept on a thin mattress on the floor. He appeared to welcome it. The worse

Diana treated him the more obedient, cowered, and she supposed ultimately, happy he seemed to be. With her resentment at the years he had spent ignoring her sexually, she found no difficulty in treating him as badly as he clearly desired.

'Charles!' she called, as she let herself into the house. She heard his bedroom door open. She started up the stairs. 'Get me a drink, then run my bath,' she said as he appeared on the landing. He set off downstairs immediately.

The bedroom had been tidied up and hoovered. Diana kicked off her shoes, and stripped off her suit and blouse for the second time that day. She could not suppress a shiver of pleasure as she remembered the first occasion. She could still feel John Borland's cock in her sex, like a phantom haunting her body.

She was down to her underwear when the timid knock interrupted her reverie.

'Come,' she said.

Charles shuffled in, set her gin and tonic with ice and lemon, on the dressing table and went to run her bath.

She slipped out of her bra and looked at her breasts in the mirror. They looked innocent, not marked or reddened, perfectly untouched except that her nipples were as hard as stone.

The gin and tonic was just what she needed. The cold liquid went straight to her head. Her mood was capricious. She went into the bathroom, drink in hand, and watched her husband bending over the bath testing the temperature of the water coming out of the mixer tap.

'Undo my stockings, Charles,' she said, on the

spur of the moment. She took another sip of the gin. He dried his hand on a towel. 'Kneel,' she ordered.

He knelt in front of her on the white tiled floor without a word. Tentatively, as though expecting a rebuke at any second, he reached out to her suspender. He pushed the little rubber knob through the metal loop releasing the nylon it held. His fingers moved to her side and unsnapped the clip there too. Then he moved to the other leg, front suspender first and then the side. Though freed, the stockings did not fall; they clung tightly to her thighs.

Diana extended her free hand to the back of Charles' head then stepped forward so his face was pressed hard into the black silk of her French knickers. She moved forward even more so his head was bent back from his spine. She could feel the bridge of his nose in her labia. He would be inhaling the musky odour of recent sex.

The gin made her feel heady. She could give him a treat. She could tell him she had just been fucked by another man, tell him all the details, how good it was, how she'd come on his finger and his cock, how he'd come inside her. She could make him go down on her, lick at her clitoris, lap at her cunt, lap up all the wetness there . . .

Her mood changed. She stepped back and released his head.

'Take my knickers down,' she said.

His hands found the waistband and pulled it down over her navel, revealing her pubic hair. It was still damp. He pulled until the knickers lay at her ankles and she stepped out of them.

'And the stockings . . .'

He rolled them down one by one. Balancing with her hand on his shoulder, she lifted each foot in turn and let him pull the stockings off.

'Now go and make sure everything's ready for Ann. Make sure everything's tidy.'

'But . . . but . . .' he said, looking crest-fallen.

'But what?' she snapped.

'I thought . . .'

'I told you this morning, Charles, in your position thinking is not a good idea.'

His erection was bulging from his trousers. She nudged it with her foot. 'Perhaps tomorrow I might let you have some release . . .'

'Really?'

'Perhaps. We'll have to see. Now go.'

He got to his feet and left, his erection bobbing out in front of him.

In the bath she finished her drink and relaxed, enjoying the residue of feelings still pleasuring her body. The drink made her drowsy and, after the excitements of the afternoon, she decided to have a nap before it was time to dress for the party.

Wrapping herself in a towelling robe she lay on the bed. Within minutes she was in a deep, dreamless sleep.

Ann was exactly on time. The doorbell rang at precisely nine thirty.

Diana had woken feeling refreshed and relaxed. She had re-done her make-up, dressed and shut Charles in his room. She answered the door herself.

'Well, look at you,' she said, admiring Ann's

dress. 'Come in, come in. You look amazing.'

They kissed on both cheeks.

Ann Connell was Diana's oldest and best friend. They had known each other since school-days. It was only recently that the relationship had become more intimate.

'I thought I'd better make an effort.' Ann said.

It was fair to describe Ann as a big woman. She was not in the least fat but tall, inches taller than Diana, and exuded a sense of physical power. Her brunette hair was cut short which suited the large features of her face. Her eyes were a fine shade of cognac brown. She made no attempt to hide her size with her choice of clothes. Tonight she wore a skintight catsuit that clung to every contour of her body as though it had been sprayed on. The black elastic material had been woven with a silvery thread so it shimmered in the light. It was clear that underneath the garment she was naked. Even the tiniest of G-strings would have shown under the cohesive catsuit.

Making no concessions to her height, Ann had completed the outfit with a pair of black patent leather spike-heeled boots.

In the living room, while Diana opened the bottle of champagne Charles had laid out in a wine cooler full of ice, Ann twirled to give her friend the full effect. Ann's arse was as large as the rest of her, two full cheeks of plump round flesh, the cleft between them enticing, a narrow valley between mountains of flesh.

'You look edible,' Diana said.

'Don't tempt me . . .' Ann replied.

'We haven't got time,' Diana chided, handing Ann

a glass of champagne. Her remark had prompted Ann's nipples to harden. Ann's breasts were not as large as Diana's but they were firm and well-shaped. The material of the catsuit flattened them slightly against her chest. It did not hide the state of her nipples.

'Cheers,' Diana said. 'I found a house.'

'Great!'

'You'll love it.' She sat down on the sofa and her friend sat next to her.

'And?'

'And what?'

'You know what.' Ann knew her friend well enough to know there was more.

Diana told her. They had always shared everything. No secrets. Diana told her everything that had happened, omitting no detail.

'Well no wonder you're looking so pleased with yourself.' Ann said, when Diana had finished.

'That's why I didn't want Charles down here.'

'Why?'

'I don't want him to know yet. About the house. I haven't decided what to do.'

'Whether to take him with you?'

'Exactly.'

'He's been well behaved hasn't he?' There was nothing Ann didn't know about Charles. Diana had told her all about him too. In fact when Diana had first told her the story of how she had discovered her husband and what he was doing, Ann had laughed so much she became a sobbing wreck doubled over on the floor.

'Oh, he hasn't put a foot wrong. It's just amazing. He's a completely different man. Or rather he's not

32

a man at all. Look at the house. It's spotless.'

'Well, I'd keep him then. Where are you going to find another housekeeper as good as him?'

'I know. It's a bit creepy though isn't it?'

'Compared with what we've seen recently. Each to his own. What difference does it make?'

It was perfectly true of course. In their work as escorts Charles' preferences were hardly rare.

'Let's not talk about him any more.' Diana put her hand on Ann's knee. The material of the catsuit felt slippery to the touch as though it were wet.

'Hadn't we better be going?'

'The car should be here any moment. I ordered it for ten. We don't want to be early do we?'

'Carolyn said this was just friends didn't she? Not business.'

'Some of her friends are clients too.'

Carolyn ran the escort agency which Diana and later, Ann, had joined.

'We'll soon see,' Ann said. She looked seriously at her friend. 'You really look great, Diana. I can't get over how much you've changed in the last few weeks.'

'We've both changed haven't we?'

'Sex, you mean?'

'No. Well, that too. But not just that. Everything's changed hasn't it? Attitudes. Life.'

'For the better.'

'Oh, definitely for better.'

'Do you know, Di, I'd love to strip that dress off you and take you to bed. Right here and now. You're so sexy. We have such wonderful times in bed.' Ann said it quite solemnly, her eyes roaming her friend's body.

Diana wore a tight red dress, no more than a tube of material into which spangles had been sewn so that they overlapped. At her bust the dress emphasised Diana's deep cleavage, as it was strapless and, at the back, it moulded itself to the firm contours of her pert pouting arse. It was short, too, so her long fine legs were visible to within inches of her crotch. They were covered in ultra sheer and almost translucent flesh-coloured tights.

Diana suppressed the wave of feeling Ann's remarks produced in her body, a delicious tingle of desire combined with a thrill of memory, at the things they had done and felt together in recent weeks. All new, fresh, wondrous.

'God we were so naïve . . .' Diana said.

'What?'

'How long ago was it?'

'The first time?'

'Yes.'

'Months.'

'I was so nervous.'

'But it was wonderful,' Ann said, turning to look in Diana's eyes. 'Wonderful. I don't think I'll ever forget that first time. I mean, however many times we do it . . .'

'Like losing your virginity . . .'

'Well it was, wasn't it?'

In a way it had been forced on them. The man Diana had been involved with, the man responsible for The Event, who'd mistaken her for an escort, had assumed she would be able to provide another girl so his boss could watch a threesome. Diana had been despondent until Ann suggested that she came along as the other girl . . .

The crunch of tyres in the drive interrupted their memories.

'Time to go,' Diana said firmly, downing the rest of the champagne in her glass.

'Just as well, this conversation was making me feel distinctly damp.'

'I have a feeling this is going to be some party.'

'Knowing Carolyn you can bet on it.'

As soon as they appeared at the front door the driver of the Daimler Princess hurried round to open the passenger door of the car and the two women climbed into the luxurious interior. He hurried back to his seat behind the wheel and slowly guided the big car out into the road.

'This is the life,' Ann said happily, squeezing Diana's hand.

Carolyn's Escort Service was ten years old to the day. It was a good excuse for a party. Carolyn Genty had made a great deal of money from her business. Enough to afford a large and secluded Victorian house in Highgate, tucked away from the road and not over-looked by prying neighbours ready to complain about the noise. Enough to throw a no-expenses-spared party. Tables were laden with cold lobsters, cans of Iranian caviar, huge Mediterranean prawns, pheasants in aspic, wild mushroom vol-au-vents; every delicacy the appetite and the heart could desire. Pretty waitresses – Carolyn had insisted on waitresses, dressed like French maids, with white caps pinned in their hair, white blouses, frou-frou skirts supported on layers of toile petticoats so short as to reveal their black suspenders and fishnet stockings – plied the assembled company with champagne or anything else they might care to partake, all of the finest quality. A small four-piece band and female vocalist played forties music in the vast living room which had been cleared to make a dance floor.

Diana and Ann had timed their arrival to perfection. The early awkwardness of any party had been dissolved by drink and almost all the guests had arrived. As the Daimler deposited them at the front door they could hear the noise of raucous laughter mixed with an up-beat version of Cole Porter's 'Let's Do It'. Diana pushed the door bell on the large panelled door. It was opened immediately.

'Darlings!' Carolyn Genty said. 'You look magnificent.'

'We thought we shouldn't under-dress,' Diana replied.

'Enter, enter.' Carolyn waved them in, kissing both in turn on each cheek.

'You look sensational,' Diana said and meant it.

Diana was always struck by Carolyn's appearance. She was a commanding figure, but her size was not like Ann's. Carolyn was more bony, her body angular, with broad sharp shoulders and pointed hips. Her dress was dramatic, a light yellow silk into which literally thousands of tiny glass beads had been sewn, the halter neck forming a collar around her throat, descending down over her bust leaving her back completely exposed. The skirt of the dress was full length and tight, shaping itself to the curves of her buttocks at the back and the slight roundness of her navel at the front. She wore her blonde hair short, cut almost like a man's.

'You probably wouldn't know any of the men here but they're all friends.'

'And customers?' Ann said pointedly.

'Some are. But strictly no business tonight. This is a party. So have a good time.'

Carolyn stopped a passing waitress and handed the two women glasses of champagne, knowing their preference. The door bell rang again and she excused herself.

Maggie, the small fragile-looking woman who ran Carolyn's office and dealt with all the appointments came over to them.

'Evening, ladies,' she said, her thick black-framed glasses giving her the air of a schoolmistress.

'Maggie, are you having a good time?'

'Ten years you know. Carolyn and I have been together for ten years.' She sounded as though she had already had quite a lot to drink.

'You were with her in the beginning then?'

'Yes,' she tapped her nose with her forefinger and lowered her voice. 'I know all Carolyn's secrets. All of them.'

'Really?' Ann said.

Maggie smiled. 'My lips are sealed.'

'Of course they are.'

Maggie, wearing the same twin-set and pearls she wore in the office, spotted someone else she wanted to greet.

'See you later . . .' she said and headed off rather unsteadily across the hallway.

Diana and Ann wandered through the reception rooms. Only two or three couples were dancing as yet and most people were helping themselves to the extensive buffet.

'I'm starving,' Ann announced.

'It looks fantastic.'

The dining room of the house had been laid out with the buffet. They queued in the small line of girls. Though there were men at the party they were greatly outnumbered by women, and a huge diversity of women at that. Most were young but there was an enormous range of sizes and types. Anything a man's heart could desire Diana thought, picturing men sitting in Carolyn's office flicking through pictures of all these women.

As they waited Diana looked around. Carolyn's taste was admirable. Everything in the house had been carefully colour co-ordinated, every chair, every picture, every ornament exactly right in its setting.

It was as they got to the plates and began to inspect the various dishes that Diana spotted Domina. She nudged Ann and indicated the distinctive Negress.

'That's her.'

'Who?'

'The girl I found Charles with.'

'Really!'

Domina spotted Diana too and came straight over. She wore a white leather cowboy outfit, a tasselled jacket and skirt with the more usual studs replaced with diamanté.

'Kirsty, isn't it?' 'Kirsty' was the name Diana had invented for herself.

'Domina, it's nice to see you. How's business?'

'Booming. It's always booming. No shortage of men who want to get their white arses whipped. Great party . . .'

38

'Great. Oh, this is Mandy. Friend of mine.'
'Mandy' was the name they had invented for Ann.

'Pleased to meet you.' Domina and Ann shook hands. 'You work for Carolyn too? If you don't you should with that body. Matter of fact you'd be a natural in my line of work. You look down on most men already.'

Ann laughed. 'That's true.'

'You could always practise on Charles,' Diana whispered, producing another giggle from Ann. 'Private joke,' she explained to Domina.

They ate and drank and talked. They drifted round the house enjoying the atmosphere, and admiring the stunning evening dresses, backless, sideless, transparent, split, or tantalising in some other way, that most of the women wore. The band went through its repertoire of Cole Porter and Ira Gershwin.

'Hello,'

The man was thirty-five and not at all handsome. His face looked as though he had been a professional boxer or a front row forward in too many rugby scrums. He was built like a rugby forward; short, stout, with no neck. But it was obvious his bulk was not fat but muscle. His head seemed to merge seamlessly into his broad shoulders. His hair was cut to within an eighth of an inch of his scalp, at least all the hair he had left, which was not a great deal.

He had addressed Ann. He stood looking up at her, the top of his head just below the level of her shoulder.

'I'm Gareth Morgan.'

'You have to be Welsh,' Ann said.

'Got it in one.'

'I'm Mandy and this is Kirsty.' They had decided to use their 'professional' names tonight.

'Pleased to meet you,' Gareth said in a lilting Welsh accent, shaking them both by the hand. His grip was strong. He only glanced cursorily at Diana before his eyes returned to Ann.

'You're a friend of Carolyn's?' Ann asked.

'Oh yes, old friend. We go back donkey's years.'

'And you play rugby. Front row.'

He looked delighted. 'You know about rugby?'

'Never miss an international Saturday. And I support Wales. Not that I'm Welsh. Just always loved the way they play.'

'My God, the girl of my dreams.'

They chatted happily together. Within minutes Ann had taken his arm, clearly more than interested in him despite their unequal size.

Leaving them to it, Diana set off to find the loo. The first floor of the house was just as tastefully decorated as the ground floor. She opened a door at the end of the corridor that looked as though it might be a bathroom. In fact it was a bedroom and it was not empty. On the small double bed a man lay completely naked, his erection pointing up vertically like a flag-pole.

To say that he was laying on the bed was not strictly true. In fact he was tied to it, spread-eagled across it. A length of white rope had been looped round his wrist and down to the leg of the bed, along to the next leg, looped round that and up to his ankle, down again to the bed leg and so on, all the way round the bed, gathering in his limbs until he was stretched taut.

Instead of closing the door again, Diana

advanced into the room for a closer look. She was
fascinated. The man was in his fifties with a large
pot-belly. His face was distended by a rubber ball
gag that bloated his cheeks like a frog. From the
gag emerged a rubber tube at the end of which was
a small orange valve and a bulb of rubber. It took
Diana a while to work out that this was what had
been used to inflate the ball of the gag once it
had been inserted in his mouth.

Diana looked into the man's eyes. He stared back
at her clearly excited by her presence. As much as
it was possible for him to do, which was hardly at
all, he stretched towards her arching his back off
the bed, pointing his cock towards her. She saw a
plea in his eyes. He wanted her to touch him. Probably more than touch. Perhaps she was not the
first woman to blunder in by mistake. Perhaps
others had come then returned with their friends
to show them what they had found.

Diana looked at his cock. It was ugly, veined and
gnarled. As she looked closely she saw a thin
leather strap had been fastened around its base
and under his balls. She felt a sudden thrill, a jolt
of sexual excitement almost like an electric shock.
But she was not tempted to do anything about it.

The disappointment registered in his eyes as she
walked away. He managed to produce a muffled
sound through the gag but it was no more than an
'ahh'. She knew it was meant to be 'please'.

Closing the door firmly behind her she opened
the next door along in the corridor. This was a big
spacious bedroom, Carolyn Genty's bedroom, and
Carolyn sat at her dressing table adjusting her
make-up.

'Kirsty . . . come in . . . just mending the damage.'

'I can't find the loo. I went next door...'

'Oh, you saw George. That'll give him a thrill.'

'He's a friend?'

'Yes, a very good friend. He's a policeman. He's been very helpful over the years.'

'That's his...?'

'It's harmless. Domina fixes him up at the beginning of the evening. He loves it. Spends all night like that. Anyone who stumbles across him, well, that's a little bonus for him. The year before last some of the girls moved the party into his room... He had quite a time.'

'Amazing.'

'And in return he watches my back. You can use my loo. It's through there.' She indicated a door at the other side of the room.

The ensuite bathroom was mainly white marble with a large circular bath and separate shower cubicle. All the fittings were white including the bidet. Diana wriggled up her dress and pulled down her tights and the tiny tanga panties she was wearing and sat on the loo.

'Are you enjoying yourself?' Carolyn shouted.

'It's great.'

Diana re-adjusted her clothes, washed her hands, brushed her hair with her fingers and came out into the bedroom. The room was luxurious. A separate dressing room to one side meant that it was uncluttered with wardrobes or chests of drawers for clothes. The only furniture was the dressing table, two modern bedside tables crafted in walnut, a television set mounted on the wall so it could be seen from the bed and a huge double bed covered with a fur counterpane. The cream carpet and beige

walls were perfectly toned. Each wall had one picture. Each picture was an oil painting of sexual
intercourse but though it appeared that the woman
being fucked was different in each, the blonde man
was the same, at least as far as Diana could tell.
It was impossible to be absolutely sure as the man's
face was not shown in any of the oils. It was always
turned away sometimes quite awkwardly.

'You like them?' Carolyn said, seeing Diana's
interest.

'Yes. They're very . . .'

'Alive?' Carolyn stood up. 'I commissioned
them . . .' Diana sensed Carolyn was about to say
more but then changed her mind.

'Say it,' she prompted.

'Oh . . .' Carolyn hesitated. 'I just wanted to say
that I find you very attractive. I hope you don't
take that the wrong way.'

'What is the wrong way?'

'Well . . . that I want to . . . that I'm trying to . . .'

'Carolyn. I'm a very grown-up lady. And I'm very
liberated. I think you're very attractive too.'

'Really?'

'Yes. Really.' Diana wanted to tell her that the
idea of Carolyn making love to her was not at all
repulsive but for the moment she thought she
would leave it at that. The night was young. Perhaps she would end it in this bedroom. Perhaps not.

'Well I better get back to being hostess. It's cabaret time.'

'Cabaret?'

'They're very good. You'll see. I think they're
incredible. But then I would.'

'What do you mean?'

43

'You'll see.'

Carolyn walked up to Diana and very slowly and deliberately took her hand in both of hers bringing it up to her lips. She kissed it with the faintest of kisses. Diana felt a frisson of passion at the lightness of the touch. She looked straight into Carolyn's very green eyes. Her face was attractive rather than beautiful; there was nothing petite about it, she had high pronounced cheekbones, large eyes, a firm symmetrical nose and chin.

The moment passed.

Diana rejoined the main party. Gareth and Ann were still together, now arm in arm.

Ten minutes later all the guests had been shepherded into the living room. A space had been cleared in front of the band and Carolyn took the vocalist's microphone.

'Ladies and gentlemen,' she said, after a roll of drums. 'Tonight, to celebrate ten years of Carolyn's Escorts . . .' There was an outburst of cheers and whoops from the assembled company. '. . . And as a special treat for you all, I'd like to present the Gresham Enigma.'

Another roll of drums and the lights all went out apart from spotlights illuminating the area that had been cleared. From behind an ornamental screen a girl emerged. She was no more than nineteen or twenty, Diana estimated, dressed in a short leather skirt and a leather halter top. Her hair was long and very black and flowed down her long back almost to the waist of the skirt. Her complexion was dark too, there was something oriental about her, perhaps Indian or Malaysian, but mixed with European blood.

The band began to play the George Harrison song, *Something*, and the girl started to dance, using her hair as a prop, swinging it round her head and over her body as she moved. After she had swept the floor with it and thrown it back and forth she started to strip. She reached behind her back and unhooked the leather halter, throwing it aside to reveal her tight firm little tits and large, very dark nipples and areole. Massaging these with both hands, while still twirling her hair in circular patterns, she moved her hips in a grinding rhythm, back and forth. Then she reached to the side of the skirt and pulled down its short zip. The zip ran the whole length of the skirt so it came away in the girl's hands. She tossed it away. Underneath, she wore a pair of crotchless tights, a neatly hemmed window exposing the whole slit of her sex; at least it would have done if she hadn't been wearing tight black panties. The panties were sewn with sequins in the shape of the Eiffel Tower. More dancing followed, the girl parting her legs and stroking her crotch or massaging her tits, or both. She ran her fingers up the sequined Eiffel Tower as if it were a cock, her thumb and forefinger following its phallic shape.

Then, looking out at the audience to seek their approval, she hooked her thumbs into the waistband of the tights.

'Yes,' the audience shouted as one.

The girl pulled the tights down over her arse. She sat on the floor, shot her legs up into the air in a jack-knife position then scissored them apart. Putting them together again she pulled the tights further down until they were hooked on the end of her toes. She pulled them taut and parted her legs again. The tights formed a catapult. The girl pulled back even further, then let go. The tights flew into the crowd. Gareth shot his hand up and plucked them from the air to a roar of applause from the room.

'They're still warm,' he said.

Ann looked at him as if he'd accomplished some death-defying feat.

The girl remained where she was on the floor. Drawing her knees up to her chin she wrapped her arms around her calves and threw her head forward so that her forehead rested on top of her knees and her long black hair formed a curtain over the front of her tightly balled body.

Immediately, another girl stepped out from behind the screen. Except it was not another girl. It was the same girl, exactly the same girl. The same hair, the same clothes. Exactly the same. The audience gasped then broke into whispered comments on how this illusion was achieved. Diana looked down at the girl on the floor. She was motionless. It must be some sort of illusion, she thought, some sort of magic act like disappearing cabinets.

The girl advanced forward. With absolute precision, she danced exactly the same steps, the same movements. She stripped her halter top off in the same way, swung her long hair in great circles, pulled the zip of the skirt at the same moment, massaged her body erotically exactly as before. It was a precise replica of what the first girl had done. Even the leather garments landed in the same spot on the side of the stage.

The reaction of the audience had turned from puzzlement to cheers and whistles of approval. When the girl stopped with her thumbs in the top of the identical sheer crotchless tights, to seek approval, the room shouted 'Yes' with even greater enthusiasm.

She drew the tights down her arse and then sat on the floor. She jack-knifed her legs, scissored them, pulled the tights to the toes, formed a catapult and shot them into the air. (Gareth did not catch them this time.) Then she drew her legs up to her chin, circled her arms round them and threw her head forward so that her hair veiled the front of her body.

The music stopped. The audience went quiet, straining to see what was going to happen next. The two identical figures were completely motionless. The drummer began a drum roll.

Diana expected one girl to simply disappear perhaps in a puff of smoke. She remembered seeing an illusion on television where there had been an explosive crack and a fog of smoke behind which the magician's assistant had vanished.

She couldn't have been more wrong. That was not the Enigma.

As the drum roll reached a crescendo both girls raised their arms straight up into the air, their fingers stretched out. They lowered them until they were vertical, until the tips of their fingers touched on one side. The audience gasped again. Like Diana, everyone had convinced themselves there was only one girl.

The saxophonist started to play and the two girls got to their feet, exactly synchronised, intertwining themselves around each other like snakes so it was impossible to tell which arm, hand, leg, foot or head belonged to which girl. They created a two-headed monster, except it was not monstrous at all, their bodies beautiful and erotic.

Diana watched with her mouth open like everyone else in the room. There was barely a sound as the audience was held spellbound by the spectacle the two girls now performed, their young bodies pressed into each other, breasts, navels, pubis, sliding, rolling, caressing their identical bodies, as the saxophone wailed to accompany their ballet.

Slowly the two parted. One of the girls, it was impossible to tell whether it was the first one who'd appeared or the second, turned to face the audience, her arms stretched apart above her head, her legs together. Her sister, since it was impossible the girls were not twins, came up behind her and pressed herself into her back. Her hands reached round to caress her throat, then dropped them to cup and squeeze her breasts. The saxophone was playing softly now and the audience heard the girl moan with pleasure. At the same time the spotlights dimmed slightly.

The hands moved to the sides of the girl's panties. The girl in front moaned and rocked her hips. The girl behind ripped at the material. Diana heard the tearing of Velcro. Immediately, the black panties fell away from the girl's pubis, though the crotch was still trapped between her legs. Her pubis was completely hairless, as smooth as the rest of her navel. The girl eased her legs apart and the panties fell to the floor. Her long delicate labia came into view.

The girl behind caressed it, wanked it, stroked it, and finally, penetrated it. The girl in front moaned rhythmically her face wreathed with pleasure. Her body undulated against her sister. After a few minutes the girl moaned to a climax, her eyes rolling back, her mouth slack, her head thrown back, a long gasp of pleasure on her lips.

As soon as she had recovered she turned her back on the audience facing her sister. Their arms wrapped around each other's backs and slowly they turned until their positions were reversed. Then the girl who had brought her sister off turned to face the audience while her sister nestled into her back and the whole procedure began again, caressing her throat, her breasts, down to the sides of her panties. It was exactly the same. The girl began to moan, little moans of pleasure, her body undulating just as her sister had done.

Diana saw the hands on the Velcro of the panties and heard its characteristic tearing. The black silk emblazoned with the sequinned Eiffel Tower fell away.

As one, the audience gasped in surprise. They were not identical twins. There, exposed, was a hairless smooth pubis just like the first girl's but hanging from its base was a small flaccid cock.

The 'girl' parted her legs and the panties fell away. Immediately the hands reached down and pulled the cock out masturbating it energetically. The saxophonist began to play loudly and fast. The cock swelled and swelled. It was as hairless as its sister's cunt had been but it was definitely a cock and was soon erect and rampant.

Coming from behind, the girl stepped in front of

the cock and straddled it with her legs, pressing her thighs together. The cock disappeared from view. There was a moan of exquisite pleasure, then a drum roll and immediately all the lights went out. There was silence and darkness.

When the lights came on both 'girls' had gone. For a long moment the silence continued. Then there was a roar of rapturous applause accompanied by whistles and whoops of approval. The whole room erupted into a babble of conversation.

'My God . . .' Diana said. 'I need a drink.'

'So do I.' Ann agreed.

'I'll get it . . .' Gareth volunteered. 'I've never seen anything like it . . .' He fought his way across to the waitresses who now stood at the doorway with trays of champagne, anticipating the need.

'That was amazing,' Ann said.

'It was a trick, wasn't it? They must both be girls.'

'It looked like a real cock to me.'

'Do you think Carolyn's got them under contract? I mean it would be quite something to have those two for the night.'

'Seventy-five per cent of the men in this room have got erections,' Diana said, looking around.

'You're right . . .' Ann grinned.

Gareth returned with the champagne. Both women stared at his fly.

'Take me a while to get over that . . .' he said, explaining what they could clearly see for themselves.

'A thousand pounds a night.' It was Carolyn. 'Everyone's asked me the same question. That's what they cost if they tickled your fancy . . .'

'Is he really a man?' Diana asked.

'That's the second question everyone's asked. What do you think?'

'I don't know.'

'That's the enigma . . .' Carolyn smiled, squeezed Diana's arm affectionately and drifted away.

The band started to play and couples began to dance. As there were comparatively few men, women were dancing together. Ann and Gareth danced, Gareth's head fitting neatly into her bosom.

Diana wandered around. The effect of the cabaret still percolated through her. She wasn't sure whether it was excitement or puzzlement or something entirely more profound, but she was in no doubt that the spectacle had affected her deeply. Apart from anything else, it had been exquisitely beautiful, especially the two bodies twined together like a statue of Shiva.

The champagne flowed, a series of deserts were served in the dining room, followed by more champagne. A giant anniversary cake was produced, cut by Carolyn with Maggie's help, and distributed to all and sundry.

Diana talked to one or two men and politely declined the inevitable passes they made at her. After her afternoon she felt no need to find a bed partner. She lost count of the number of glasses of champagne she drank.

People gradually began to drift away. The rooms slowly emptied. Diana decided to go too and looked around for Ann. But Ann had disappeared.

Carolyn was at the front door seeing people off.

'I think it's time I went,' Diana said. 'Have you seen Ann?'

'She's staying the night.' Carolyn replied, smiling.

'Is she?'

'I think so. She's upstairs.'

'Alone?'

'Of course not. Why don't you stay too? There's lots of room.'

'No, I think I'll go home.'

She could see a flash of disappointment on Carolyn's face. 'I'd hoped you'd stay. I wanted to talk to you.'

'I think I'm a bit drunk.'

It was true. The fresh air from the front door had hit her and she realised she had definitely overdone the champagne.

'That was the idea. Come with me. I'll get you some coffee.'

Carolyn lead Diana to the huge kitchen and sat her down. One of the waitresses plied her with coffee and a glass of sparkling water, while Carolyn returned to the front door to see people off. By the time the front door had closed for the last time Diana felt sober again or, at least, less woozy.

Waitresses busied themselves bringing in dishes from the buffet and washing up. Carolyn returned.

'That was the last.'

'I should go.'

'Stay.' Carolyn knelt by Diana's chair. 'Are you feeling better?'

'Much.'

'Then stay.'

The prospect of returning home on her own was suddenly not very appealing. 'It was a great party, Carolyn.'

'It was, wasn't it? Come on. Let's leave them to it.'

Carolyn took her hand and led her through the house and up the stairs.

'I should go...' Diana said as they got to the landing. She half-meant it.

'No you shouldn't,' Carolyn said quietly, but firmly, pulling her hand and leading her towards the bedroom.

But in the luxurious bedroom Diana's hesitancy vanished. She began to feel in control of herself again, the effect of the alcohol wearing off.

'That was the most extraordinary act I've ever seen,' she said.

Carolyn had produced two large glasses of sparkling water from somewhere.

'Here,' she said handing Diana a glass and drinking her own until it was empty. 'Yes, they're amazing aren't they?'

'And they're on your books?' Diana drank the water thirstily, despite all the water she had drunk in the kitchen.

'Yes.'

'Is it a trick? Are they both women?'

'No. Definitely not... I...' She stopped herself.

'What?'

'I... I have special reasons for thinking it's rather moving. Profound.'

'If affected me too and I don't know the reason.'

'Diana...' Carolyn said seriously.

'Yes?'

'If you want to just sleep that's fine. If you want to sleep alone that's fine too. There are other rooms upstairs...'

'Carolyn. I told you, I'm a big girl.' Diana finished the water. She felt completely revived now. 'I'm quite sober. Why don't you ask me what I'd really like?' She brought the back of her hand up to touch Carolyn's cheek. Carolyn looked worried and apprehensive.

'What would you really like?'

'For us to climb into that big bed of yours together and make wild passionate love.'

'Oh Diana, I want to please you. I want to give you pleasure. That's all I want. Do you understand?'

'As long as it won't affect our business relationship,' Diana joked. After all she was about to sleep with the boss.

'It won't, but that's not what I meant. I have to do this on my own terms. It's difficult for me to explain . . .'

'Don't say anything else . . .'

Diana took the glass from Carolyn's hand and set it next to hers on the dressing table. She moved her hand up to Carolyn's bare shoulder, trailing it along her skin until it reached the back of her neck. Then she moved forward to kiss her, pressing her mouth down on to her lips. As their tongues met she suddenly felt a flame of passion shoot up through her body. Up to that point Diana had felt curiously detached, knowing Carolyn wanted her, and going along with the idea almost mechanically. Earlier, she had felt attracted to Carolyn but that feeling had temporarily vanished, perhaps through the effects of too much champagne. But now it returned with a vengeance. She felt attraction turn to lust as Carolyn's arms wrapped round her, drawing her into an embrace as her tongue thrust into her mouth.

Diana closed her eyes. In the blackness there, she saw the flames of the log fire and felt John Borland's cock hard against her navel.

Carolyn broke the kiss and the embrace.

'Excuse me.' She said. There was an expression on her face Diana could not read but it seemed to be part shyness, part embarrassment. Carolyn went into the bathroom and closed the door.

Diana pulled the tube of spangled material over her head, unpinned her long hair, kicked off her high heels with some relief, and shucked herself out of her tights and panties. She brushed her hair with the small brush from her evening bag and, naked, walked up to each of the oil paintings in turn. She examined them closely. They were marvellous pictures, the flesh of the models almost alive, their sex seemingly throbbing with life, but the fact that the man's face was always obscured somehow appeared artificial, as though imposed on the artist by his model.

The bathroom door opened and Carolyn appeared. Much to Diana's surprise she was wearing a peach coloured nightdress, a satiny material with lace panels at the bottom and each side. Under the nightdress, even more surprisingly, Diana could clearly see the outline of a pair of knickers. The knickers were not brief but rather old-fashioned like a pantie-girdle. Carolyn threw back the fur counterpane and climbed into bed. The bed was made with cream silk sheets. Diana slipped in beside her.

'Sorry to have been so long,' Carolyn said. She turned to a lamp on the bedside table, identical to the lamp on the other side of the bed, and moved a small gnarled switch on its base. Both lamps dimmed.

Carolyn turned to take Diana in her arms, pressing her mouth down into a kiss, then kissing her throat and her shoulders. Her mouth felt hot and wet. It kissed and sucked and lapped at Diana's flesh, down to her breasts, over their high arch until it found her hard corrugated nipples.

'Beautiful,' Carolyn said before attaching the nipple to her mouth like a limpet.

Diana moaned. Carolyn's fingers found the other nipple. While her mouth manipulated one, the tips of her fingers and her well-manicured nails worked on the other. She was not gentle, she pinched them, stretched them, pressed them. Diana could feel herself getting aroused, feel her juices beginning to flow. She kicked back the sheet and opened her legs, feeling for Carolyn's body with her thigh.

Carolyn was lying on her side. Diana rubbed against the silk of the nightdress, her thigh pressing into Carolyn's lap. She could only feel the silkiness of the two layers of material that sheathed her sex.

Carolyn's mouth moved down to Diana's flat belly. She moved herself away from Diana's probing leg, coming up on to her knees as her mouth reached the triangular forest of pubic hair. Diana felt her hot breath. She arched her body up off the bed desperately wanting the touch of Carolyn's mouth on her throbbing sex, not caring, for the moment, why Carolyn was so modestly dressed. She felt Carolyn's tongue lapping out, teasing her by drawing long lines on her thighs, like an artist's brush, up and down, almost to her knee, then back up, up almost to her labia but not quite.

'Please, please . . .' Diana said, her voice deep with her need.

Carolyn gave her what she wanted. She sunk her whole mouth on to Diana's sex, as if it was a mouth, kissing it like a mouth, moving her lips against it, darting her tongue out to penetrate deep into Diana's cunt. Diana moaned involuntarily. She had never felt a tongue go so deep. It was hot and she could feel its roughness reaming into her, lapping at her copious juices. Then it pulled away and was nudging at her clitoris.

Diana knew she was going to come. Carolyn's tongue was doing the things she loved. It was no more than two months since she had first gone to bed with a woman. It had astonished her how much pleasure a woman could give her. It astonished her still. She was so glad she had discovered these pleasures, these secret pleasures hidden in a veil of taboos.

Her body tensed. Every muscle locked tight, waiting and wanting release. Carolyn's tongue moved rhythmically, remorselessly. Diana felt her hand on her thigh, moving up to the lips of her cunt, and knew what she was going to do. As the tongue worked on her clitoris she felt Carolyn's finger searching for the opening of her sex, then plunging inside, one finger, two, then three, filling her. They delved deep without disturbing the rhythm of her tongue.

Diana's orgasm began. She felt the first sensation flooding through her but instead of an explosion it hit her in waves, wave after wave crashing through her body, centred on the tiny movements of the tip of Carolyn's tongue and the fingers literally crammed into her cunt. It went on and on and on, her body tossed, racked by overwhelming sensation, unable to do anything, to think anything, only surrender to her passion.

Carolyn sensed the moment the orgasm passed. Very gently she pulled her fingers out and moved her tongue away.

'Oh, darling...' Diana managed to say.

'You're so beautiful...' Carolyn said, looking down at Diana's nakedness, her legs spread apart, her breasts falling to either side of her chest, their nipples as hard as cherry stones.

'So good,' Diana said quietly, as control returned to her body. She looked up at Carolyn who still knelt beside her. The lace of the nightdress hid her breasts. 'Take that off, I want to see you.'

'Diana...' Carolyn's voice was full of emotion.

'Please...' Diana said, not understanding the expression on Carolyn's face.

'I...' Carolyn stopped herself. Then, with obvious reluctance, she drew the nightdress over her head. Her breasts were small, no more than a purse of flesh balanced on her ribs. Her nipples were small too.

Diana sat up and kissed both nipples delicately as though saying hello. Then she gathered one between her lips and pinched it with her teeth. Carolyn moaned. Diana, without letting go of the nipple, pushed her back on to the bed.

'No...' Carolyn said, as Diana's hands began to caress her body. 'No. I didn't mean for you to...'

'Yes...' Diana said in a whisper.

Diana worked on her breasts. Taking her mouth

away she kneaded and massaged both breasts with her hand, pinching the nipples, rolling the flesh round, making Carolyn moan again.

Diana got to her knees, her big breasts quivering as she moved. She ran her hand down Carolyn's body to the waistband of her knickers. They were tight, made of an elasticated material, and came right up to her waist. As soon as Diana started to pull them down Carolyn's hand stopped her.

'No ... I wanted to make love to you ...'

'Now it's your turn.'

'No ... I can't ...'

'Why, Carolyn? I want to. I want to badly.'

'Please Diana. I'm very ... I'm not like other women down there ... I'm very ugly.'

'I don't mind that.'

'It's so ugly. I hate it ...'

'I want to. Please let me Carolyn ... I don't mind whatever it looks like.'

Diana looked straight into Carolyn's green eyes. She could see she was trying to decide what to do. Then, her decision apparently made, she released Diana's hand and turned to switch off the dimmed lights.

The room was pitch black. No light leaked through the curtains from the street lamps outside.

Diana pulled on the waistband of the knickers and felt Carolyn arch her hips off the bed so she could strip them down to her thighs. It was a struggle to get them off. Finally, Diana wrestled them down to Carolyn's slim ankles and over her feet. Delicately she kissed the top of Carolyn's foot, lifting it to her mouth. She kissed her calf and her knee and her thigh. She went back to the foot on the other leg and did the same, working her way up the leg with little pecking kisses.

Diana's feeling of lust had been replaced almost entirely by curiosity. She had no idea what to expect. Her eyes had adjusted in the dark enough for her to see the outline of Carolyn's angular body but nothing more.

'You don't have to...' Carolyn said, her head turned to one side and pressed into the pillow.

'I want to...' Diana answered.

As her mouth worked on Carolyn's thighs, moving across them both, kissing and licking, her hand caressed her navel, making little circles on it with her palm, gradually working her hand lower until she could feel the side of her little finger brushed by pubic hair.

Then Diana took the plunge. She pushed her fingers downwards into Carolyn's pubic triangle. Her pubic hair was thick, curly and very wiry and harsh. And then she found it, down at the apex of the triangle, instead of the cleft of labia, Diana's fingers wrapped around a slim, flaccid stem of what was undoubtedly a cock.

'It's so ugly...' Carolyn said as she felt Diana's fingers examining the unwanted appendage. 'I've never had the courage to have surgery...'

Diana tried not to be fazed. She caressed the cock with her hands but it remained soft.

'What do I do to please you?' she asked softly. She was in so far now there was no point turning back. She felt no disgust, nor did she feel pity. Her overwhelming desire was to give Carolyn some pleasure.

'I take hormones. It's shrunk a lot...'

Diana kissed her on the mouth, hard, pushing her tongue down between Carolyn's lips, wanting to make her feel good. As she broke away she said firmly, 'Shh...'

She moved her head down to Carolyn's lap. Her hands fed it into her mouth. She heard Carolyn groan. Her fingers groped between Carolyn's legs to find the balls. They were small too, no more than little oval pebbles. She squeezed them, then abandoning the cock, sucked the balls instead. Carolyn groaned again, louder this time.

Diana felt a wave of excitement. It was all so bizarre but it was thrilling. It did not disgust her, it excited her, it excited her in exactly the same way the cabaret had excited her. And now she knew Carolyn's special reason for finding that so moving.

Almost without thinking, obeying her instincts, she swung her legs over Carolyn's head so her cunt was poised above Carolyn's mouth. Carolyn didn't need any prompting. She raised her head, wrapped her arms around Diana's thighs, and clamped her lips to Diana's hairy sex, lapping immediately at her clitoris, licking her labia, probing the opening of her cunt as she had done before. Diana, in turn, took the cock back into her mouth. She worked her hands under Carolyn's thighs until she could feel the bud of her anus. Without hesitation she pushed a finger into it, right up as far as it would go, right up to her knuckle. She felt Carolyn's reaction – a shock of hot air against her cunt as Carolyn gasped with pleasure.

The cock had swollen slightly. She used her finger

to fuck Carolyn, moving it in and out while Carolyn attacked her clitoris. Diana felt her heavy breasts hanging down, their nipples on Carolyn's navel. She could feel herself starting to come again, her mind full of extraordinary images, seeing Carolyn at the party in her yellow dress, so beautiful, so elegant, seeing Carolyn's face, seeing her in a man's clothes, her face made-up, imagining her as a man. These thoughts were making her come.

But she wanted to control it. She wanted this to be Carolyn's turn. She wanted, needed Carolyn's pleasure.

The cock was swelling again, but was by no means erect. With her free hand Diana gathered in the balls and squeezed them. Again she felt Carolyn's gasp expelling hot air against her clitoris. She sucked harder on the cock, squeezed tighter on the balls and pushed her finger deeper. At once her efforts were rewarded, the cock spasmed in her mouth and she tasted the saltiness of spunk. It did not spit out, but trickled. There was not much of it. Not that this seemed to matter to Carolyn whose whole body was convulsing with feeling.

Somehow, through it all, she managed to keep her mouth on Diana's cunt. She, in turn, was rewarded for the effort. Freed of the necessity to control herself, Diana let the orgasm she had held back explode in her body, let all the wild and wonderful images coalesce into a volcano of sensation. Her mind and her body came together – the feelings in her body in tune with the images in her mind. Her whole body trembled as Carolyn's artful tongue came to rest.

Diana rolled over on to her back. There was a

long silence. Their heartbeats returned to normal, their breathing became regular again.

'That felt so good,' Carolyn said, at last. 'You had no need to do that. I just wanted to give you pleasure.'

'Carolyn. I told you. I wanted to. It doesn't matter does it?'

'I've never let anyone do that before.'

'If you want the truth I found it exciting. I was excited by the cabaret so it's no surprise I suppose.'

'Were you?'

'Yes. Why shouldn't I be?'

'You made it exciting for me. You're a remarkable woman, Diana. No wonder you're so popular with the clients.'

'And you're a remarkable woman too, Carolyn,' Diana said. They both laughed.

It was true, however. Diana could not and would not ever be able to think of Carolyn as anything but a woman.

Chapter Three

Diana slept badly. It may have been sleeping in a
strange bed or all the excitements of the day – it
had, after all, been a very full day, from finding the
house to her experience with Carolyn. Whatever
the reason, Diana slept fitfully, her mind replay-
ing the events of the day unable to unwind. Carolyn, on the other hand, had lapsed into a deep and
apparently peaceful sleep.

At five in the morning Diana decided to get herself a glass of milk. Milk, she had read, was good
at soothing over-excited nerves. Slipping out of bed
as quietly as she could, she tiptoed across the room,
wrapped a bathrobe she found hanging on the bedroom door around her body, and made her way
downstairs to the kitchen.

Most of the party mess had been washed up and
cleared away but there was still the debris of black
rubbish sacks. Diana found a large American-made
refrigerator and helped herself to a bottle of milk.
She searched the cupboards for a glass.

'Great minds think alike.'

The voice made Diana start. She almost dropped
the milk. Ann stood by the kitchen door. Exactly
like her friend, she was dressed in a bathrobe.

'Couldn't sleep,' Diana explained. 'Milk?'

Ann nodded. 'I thought you'd gone home.'

Diana poured the milk into two glasses she'd discovered in one of the wall cupboards. 'I got seduced. And so, obviously, did you.'

'And how! God, Diana, that guy's amazing. His cock's so thick.'

'Thick?'

'Wide. Round.' Ann made a circle by touching the fingers and thumbs of her hands together. 'I mean it's not particularly long but it's like a tree trunk. I came just while he was trying to get into me. I'm a bit sore actually. Nice sore though.' Ann rubbed her thighs together to see if the soreness was still there. It was. 'And what about you then?'

'Oh. Let's say I had a very interesting time.' Diana had no intention of gossiping to all and sundry about Carolyn but there was no way she was not going to tell her friend.

'Who? I didn't see you with anyone.'

'Tell you tomorrow.'

'It is tomorrow.'

'Tell you when we get home.'

Ann gave up and drunk the milk. 'Back to bed, then,' she said. 'Hey,' she suddenly added, 'why don't you come?'

'Come where?'

'To bed. Gareth's asleep. Let's give him a little surprise.'

Diana smiled. 'No . . . I think . . .'

'Oh, come on. It's a party. He'll think it's his birthday.'

Diana finished the milk and put the glass down on the kitchen counter. For the life of she could not think of one good reason why she shouldn't go with Ann. Her body was already tingling with the idea and these days she had learnt to listen to what her body wanted her to do. Besides she was intrigued by Ann's description.

'Why not,' she said.

'Listen, this is what we'll do ...'

They devised a plan.

Upstairs they crept past Carolyn's room and up to the second floor. As quietly as they could, the two women tiptoed into the bedroom Ann had been given. Gareth lay on the bed. He was covered by a single sheet, the heating in the house having been left on and the room warm. Ann pulled the sheet away. As the curtains had not been drawn, the room was lit by the orange glow of the street lights outside and Diana could see Gareth's stout but powerful body. His thighs and upper arms were particularly well developed, knotted and veined with muscle. They pulled off their robes.

As planned, Ann slid on to the bed next to him, while Diana knelt on the other side by his navel. She took his flaccid cock in her hand and started wanking it, slowly pulling back his foreskin.

'Darling ...' Ann whispered. 'Wake up, darling. I'm so randy again.'

'Ammm ...' he murmured, turning his head towards her though still half asleep.

'I'm randy, darling ...' Ann said, like a little girl who wanted to be allowed to play with her favourite doll.

'Ammm ...'

Ann kissed him on the mouth, gently at first then harder using the kiss to wake him up. Diana, meanwhile, continued to manipulate his cock.

'That's nice,' he said, when Ann's mouth relented.

'Is it darling. Do you like me wanking you?' Ann said.

Before he could answer she gagged him with her mouth again forcing her tongue between his lips.

His cock was hard now and Diana could see what Ann had meant. Though it was a normal length its circumference was massive. It looked out of proportion, like the stub of a felled tree. Diana wondered if her mouth was wide enough to take it.

Leaning forward she positioned herself above his cock then plunged her lips down onto it, managing to circle it with no trouble. It tasted of Ann, a taste Diana knew well.

'Ammm . . .' Gareth moaned into Ann's mouth.

Both women waited for the penny to drop. It was like an intelligence test. How long would it take him to work out that the mouth sucking his cock could not be Ann's?

'What!' he said, pushing Ann away. Diana did not withdraw but looked at him in the half-light. He started to laugh. 'This I have to see . . .'

He reached for the bedside lamp and switched it on.

'Gareth, this is my friend Diana. You met downstairs, remember?'

By way of 'hello' Diana sucked harder on his cock and made Gareth moan.

'I told her you had a very special cock and as we share everything . . .'

'She's so good at that . . .'

'She wants to fuck you, Gareth. While I watch.

Does that turn you on?' Ann whispered in his ear.

'Are you joking?' Diana felt his cock surge.

Lifting her head from his cock, Diana swung her legs over his body so she sat on her haunches, her cunt poised over his cock.

'Hello, Gareth,' she said, running her hands over his hairless chest.

'Hello, again,' he said, still not believing his luck and wondering if he were going to wake up from an elaborate wet dream. Ann had been luck enough. He had sucked and fucked that big body of hers to his heart's content. And now this. He didn't think he'd ever felt his cock so hard.

'Are you going to fuck me?' Diana asked. She could feel the heat of his cock it was so close to her labia. She could feel the wetness flowing in her body.

'Yes, yes . . .' he said.

'Yes.' She sunk down on him. Though his cock entered her it did not go all the way in. He was too thick. She eased herself off then pushed down again. It took three strokes before he was in, before she could feel the base of his cock on her clitoris and before she realised her body was so stretched, her clitoris so exposed by the fact that her labia were so fully opened that she was coming, coming hot and strong over this incredible cock.

'Oh, God, oh, my God . . .' She couldn't control herself, her whole body was trembling, her tits quivering. She would never have believed she could respond this way after all the sex she had had. But she was. Gareth reached up and cupped her tits in his hands squeezing them tightly.

'Great tits . . .' he mumbled, almost to himself.

She eased herself off his cock when she thought her orgasm had run its course but it hadn't. That motion made her come again, made her sink back on to him, made her want to feel stretched open again, her clitoris on fire with sensation, as though pulled taut like the string of an instrument, strung tight and played.

She felt Ann come round to hold her shoulders, holding her down, holding her steady. She would have loved to kiss Ann's mouth, the mouth she knew so well, but there was no way she could concentrate on anything but the feelings from her cunt and the knot of her clitoris.

Ann knew what she was feeling. She had felt it all herself.

It seemed like forever before Diana's senses returned. Ann felt her body relax. 'See . . .' she whispered.

'Oh, God yes . . .' Diana managed to gasp.

Gareth was smiling. He was used to the effect he had on women. Slowly he started moving his cock inside Diana's wet cunt. She moaned. He could feel her juices running down his hard stem and out over his balls. He bucked his hips and began to fuck her harder and faster concerned for himself now and not for her. He watched as Ann kissed her friend's neck then moved down to those magnificent tits. He saw her cup them in her hand, draw the nipples into her mouth, one at a time. Then he felt her hand reach under Diana's buttocks to find his balls. Ann was kneeling with her back to him now. He moved his hand down between Ann's legs and thrust his fingers up into her labia until he found her cunt. He had never felt that before. His hand in one cunt, his cock in another.

Ann pulled at his balls. He kept his eyes open for as long as he could, wanting to memorise the image of the two women. Ann was using one hand to knead and paw at Diana's breast while the other played with his balls; juggling them, squeezing them, pulling them away from his cock. She was bouncing up and down on his hand too, wanting it moving in and out of her sex.

Suddenly he felt a new sensation. A finger was moving on his cock. How could it be? He felt it distinctly. It was making him come, finally taking him over the edge. As he lost the battle to keep his eyes open he realised what Ann had done. In his mind's eye he could see her finger pushed deep into Diana's anus, wanking him through the thin wall, making him come. Then he could see nothing. He could only feel, as his spunk jetted out into Diana's willing cunt.

'Hello,' Diana answered the phone. It was twelve o'clock.

'Hi.' It was Maggie. She sounded less than her usual bouncy self.

'Hung over?'

'And how. You?'

'No. I think I worked it off.'

'Good, 'cause I've got a job for you.'

'Fire away.' Diana picked up the pencil she kept by the phone. She opened her little notepad.

'Very short notice.'

'That's OK.'

'One o'clock.'

'It's twelve now.'

'I know. Hamilton Grill. The guy wants a lunch companion. Name of Fraser. Ronald Fraser. He's a regular.'

'What's he into?'

'It varies.' Maggie said. 'All harmless. None of the girls have complained.

'I'd better get my skates on then. Is it smart there?'

'Very.'

'I'll make it. Just. Better fly. Hope you feel better soon.'

'Well at least I'll die happy.'

Diana rushed upstairs, changed into a navy blue suit and cream blouse with the first set of decent lingerie that came to hand, underneath. It was probably unnecessary but she liked to be prepared for any eventuality. She called a cab. It would take too long to find somewhere to park and still be there on time.

The cab deposited her outside the Hamilton Grill at five past one. A uniformed commissionaire held the door open for her and she walked into the restaurant.

Maggie had been right. It was very smart and looked as though it had recently been redecorated. Everything was rich and plush. The bar, its walls covered in beige-coloured suede, held sturdy leather armchairs with round tables individually lit by halogen spotlights set in a brass track overhead. A long black laquered counter ran the whole length of the room and behind it, back-lit by a diffuse fluorescent light, were, as well as the more work-a-day bottles of booze, a collection of tastefully arranged single malts and ageing Cognacs and Armagnacs.

Diana walked up to the little desk where the maître d' was fussing over his reservations book.

'Mr Ronald Fraser?' she said.

'Yes, madam. Follow me please.'

With an extravagant gesture of the hand he indicated the bar and then led Diana through the maze of armchairs to the far side where a small, immaculately dressed man in his early sixties sat nursing a glass of malt whisky.

'Mr Fraser?' Diana said.

'Charmed,' the man said, standing up. He took her hand and kissed it lightly. 'Thank you, Alberto ...' he nodded to the maître d' who made another hand gesture which presumably meant 'not at all,' and walked back to his station.

Ronald Fraser concentrated on Diana. His eyes took in her face, the slight suggestion of cleavage the blouse allowed under her buttoned jacket, her slim waist, and her finely shaped calves and spiky high heels.

'Charmed,' he repeated, this time as a verdict on what he saw. Then, as if realising he had been staring too long, 'Please, how rude of me, please sit down ... A drink before lunch?'

'Thank you. What is it you're drinking?'

'Malt whisky. They have rather a good collection here. This is Lagavulin from the Western Islands, from Islay actually. It's a very distinct taste.'

'I'd like to try that.' Diana sat down in the leather armchair opposite. She saw his eyes follow the movement. As she crossed her legs his eyes darted down hoping for a glimpse of thigh. Diana's skirt was too long for him to see anything but a pair of neatly crossed knees.

He caught the waiter's attention and made a sign which he seemed to understand.

'You are a very beautiful young woman,' he said seriously.

'And you are a handsome man,' she replied. It was true. Ronald Fraser, though short, was well-proportioned and attractive. His firm symmetrical features were complemented by soft brown eyes. His hair, parted and combed, had hardly receded at all though it was almost entirely grey. Diana noticed his hands. His fingers were long and thin and articulate as though used to perform incredibly difficult tasks of dexterity.

'Have you had to come far?'

'Not really.'

'Short notice, I'm afraid. I just thought I'd give myself a little treat.'

'And why not?'

'Exactly.'

The waiter brought her drink and two menus. When he had gone she sipped the golden liquid experimentally. It tasted quite different from any whisky she had tasted before.

'The malts are just as individual as wines. The Western Islands are the most distinctive of all. They say it's because the peat is made up of a high proportion of seaweed.'

'It's very smooth.'

'Now, what would you like to eat?'

'Oysters and Dover sole.' Diana said without looking at the menu. 'Grilled Dover sole.'

'You like oysters?'

'I love them.'

'Few women do.'

He called the waiter back and ordered a dozen

oysters each. He too had a grilled Dover sole. He chose a Premier Cru Chablis from the wine list and ordered Perrier.

'That's that taken care of,' he said finishing his drink. 'An ideal lunch.'

'So, Mr Fraser . . .' Diana said.

'Ronnie . . .'

'So, Ronnie, what can I do for you?'

He reached into his jacket pocket and extracted a cream envelope made from a heavy vellum. He passed it across to her. The envelope was not sealed. Diana could see five fifty-pound notes neatly aligned inside.

'Is that satisfactory?'

'Perfectly.'

'What colour knickers are you wearing?' he said in exactly the same tone of voice that he'd used to order the food.

Diana looked into his eyes. She could see the spark of excitement there.

'Black.'

'What type are they?'

'Bikini knickers. They're cut very high on the hip, practically up to the waist. I have very long legs. They make them look longer.'

She heard Fraser sigh. 'I'm sure they do.'

Diana unbuttoned her jacket. Her blouse showed a little of the cleavage formed by her underwired bra. His eyes fell to her chest. She ran a finger along the neck line of the blouse, just touching the naked swelling of her breasts.

'And your bra?' he asked.

'I shouldn't have worn a black bra under a cream blouse, should I?'

'Why not?'

75

'It shows. I mean you can see it, can't you?'

'Only the outline.'

'I should wear white really.'

'I suppose so.'

'I have very big tits. Heavy. I'd like to not have to wear a bra. Let them loose, but they're just too big. They need support.'

'I can see that.'

'I prefer black. It's so sexy don't you think?'

'Yes. Do you wear your tights over your knickers or underneath?' His eyes had narrowed. He was looking at her knees now. Diana uncrossed her legs and did not re-cross them. She let her knees part slightly.

At that moment the waiter announced that their table was ready.

'Right. We'll be right there.'

The waiter hurried away.

'Shall we go through?'

'Yes, you've made me quite hungry,' Diana said.

They got up together and Fraser took her arm. His erection tented the front of his trousers. He put his hand in his pocket to flatten it against his belly as he walked.

They strolled out of the bar into the restaurant. Here too the decor had a feel of understated wealth and prestige. A thick burgundy carpet matched the upholstery of the dining chairs, crisp white linen on all the tables, napkins starched into the shape of a fan, small sprigs of flowers in a silver vase on each table, waiters dressed in white shirts and black trousers, little linen aprons tied around their waists in the French style – not surprisingly since all the staff was French.

76

Ronald Fraser was obviously a regular customer. Waiters bowed and greeted him by name as they progressed through the room. Two waiters pulled out the chairs at his table, which was the best in the restaurant, a corner from which everyone else could be seen. As soon as they were seated, they snapped the napkins in the air and trailed them over their customer's laps.

'Where were we?' Diana said, as the waiter poured the Chablis for Fraser to try.

'Tights,' he said apparently with no embarrassment. 'That's fine,' he said to the waiter.

'I don't wear tights,' Diana said.

The waiter poured the light golden wine into Diana's glass. He gave no indication of understanding the conversation though Diana was sure he did. 'I wear stockings. Much sexier.'

But the waiter's hand trembled at this remark and three or four drops of the wine spilt on the cloth. He mopped them up hurriedly and took the bottle to Fraser's glass.

'So you're wearing a suspender belt?'

'Of course.'

'Black?'

'Yes.'

The waiter's hand was trembling again. He spilt more wine.

'*Je me pardonne.*'

'*De rein.*' Fraser said in a perfect French accent.

The waiter hurried away, his command of English evidently extending to more than restaurant matters.

'We scared him I think,' Fraser said.

'Or turned him on.'

'You've turned me on.'

'I noticed.'

'Why do you wear stockings rather than tights? Most women wear tights nowadays don't they?'

'I suppose so. But they're awfully restricting. I like to feel free. I like to feel my naked thighs. It makes me feel sexy. That band of nylon half-way up my thigh and then all that creamy naked flesh above it. The stockings make it seem much more exposed somehow, more naked ... Do you know what I mean?' Diana touched his hand on the table. She saw him looking down at her legs as if trying to imagine what she looked like sitting there in her suspenders. 'I always wear very sheer nylons too, the ones with Lycra. They look slippery, shiny. Are you hard again?'

'Again,' he smiled. 'I've been hard since we left the bar. You're a remarkable woman. You catch on very quickly don't you?'

It was the second time in twenty-four hours that Diana had been called 'remarkable'. 'Catch on?'

'To what is required. You are obviously very instinctive.'

'Do you want to know a secret?'

'Yes.'

'Why I'm good at it?'

'Yes.'

'Because I love it.' He didn't need to be convinced. He could see from the excitement in her eyes that what she said was true. Their conversation had turned her on as much as it had him.

'When did you last make love?' he asked.

Diana looked at her watch. 'Fuck, you mean. Seven hours ago.'

78

'Really?' he leant forward in his seat. The table was round, larger than a table for two, so they were seated almost side by side. 'That was very early this morning.'

'Yes. Carolyn had a party.'

'And you were fucked?' He made 'fucked' sound like a medical word, like an appendectomy.

Two waiters arrived carrying silver platters on which the opened oysters rested on a bed of crushed ice. They set the platters down in front of their customers.

'Yes,' Diana said, ignoring the waiters again.

'More than once?'

'Brown bread, madam?' The waiter was offering Diana a plate of thinly sliced, buttered, brown bread.

'No,' she said. 'Thank you.'

'No,' Fraser said, before he could be asked.

'I was only *fucked* once . . .' Diana said accurately.

'But . . .' he'd picked up the emphasis in her voice that indicated that 'fucked' was not all that had happened.

A waiter arrived now with a plate of lemons, cut in half and wrapped in muslin. He put them down in the middle of the table as Diana continued.

'I was in bed with a woman before that.'

'Tabasco? Vinegar?' the waiter asked.

'Nothing, thank you,' Fraser said.

'Thank you, sir.' The waiter appeared reluctant to leave and miss the rest of the conversation but he clearly had no choice.

'You are into women then?'

'Yes.'

'Are you a lesbian?'

Diana laughed. 'No. But I like to have sex with women.'

'More than men.'

'No. Equal. Not even equal, it's just different. I like sex. All sex.'

'Will you touch me?'

'Now?'

'Yes.'

'Anything you want.'

With one hand she squeezed lemon juice over an oyster, then slipped it into her mouth; with the other she reached under the tablecloth to find his thigh. She walked her fingers up to his lap and grasped his erection, pinching it hard.

'Tell me about being fucked. Was it good?' Fraser ate an oyster too.

'Very. It was my friend's idea.'

'Your friend?'

'Yes. She'd met this man at the party.' Under the table Diana found the top of the zip to his flies and pulled it down. 'We thought we'd give him a treat.'

'So it was a threesome.'

'Yes. She massaged his balls while I fucked him.'

'You were on top?'

'Yes.' She ate another oyster. She fished inside the zip. There was the tail of his shirt and various other clothing but she couldn't find his naked flesh.

'What is your fantasy? Tell me what you would really like? I mean if you could do anything?'

'I think I could be quite kinky.' Diana's fantasies had all come true, she had done everything she had

80

ever dreamt of doing in the last weeks.

'Kinky?' He sat forward again resting on his elbows, his fingers laced together.

Diana ate an oyster. Her hand found the fly of his pants and pulled his cock out through his zip. She covered it with his napkin.

'Would you excuse me a moment?' she said.

He looked surprised then genuinely concerned. 'Are you all right?'

'Perfectly. I've just had an idea. I'll be back in a minute. Don't you dare put it away.'

Immediately he saw her start to stand up, a waiter came to pull her chair back. He escorted her to a door marked LADIES and stationed himself outside to wait for her. His wait was much shorter than he'd imagined. Almost before the door was closed Diana was out again.

At the table he pushed her chair forward as she sat down.

'Thank you,' she said.

'My pleasure.' He walked away.

'Now ...' She put her hand back under the tablecloth. Balled up in her palm were her black knickers. She wrapped them round his still-rampant cock. 'My knickers,' she told him. 'Can you feel them? They're still warm. They're damp too. All this talk's made me wet.'

'Oh ...' Fraser shuddered as he felt the warm silky material being rubbed against the soft flesh of his circumcised cock.

'Oh ... So good, darling.'

'Yes ...' She slipped another oyster in her mouth without breaking the rhythm she had started on his cock. Then she lent over and forked one up off

Fraser's plate and popped it into his mouth.

'Do you want me to tell you my fantasy? I mean what would really turn me on?'

'Yes . . .' he said, feeling her hand wanking him quite aggressively.

She fed him another oyster. The waiter who had wanted to listen to their conversation had stationed himself near their table. The restaurant was quiet with only a few other tables occupied. Nearest to their table a party of six men, conservatively dressed and all over fifty, were paying no attention to them. But the waiter was.

'Do my knickers feel good?'

'Tell me your fantasy.'

'What I'd really like . . . It would be here, in this room . . .' She squeezed and pummelled his hard sword of flesh. 'I'd be here with all these waiters. All these men.' She saw the waiter watching her. He would have to be very stupid not to realise what was happening under the tablecloth. 'It would be like a dream, like I'd been running away from someone in a dream and all these waiters would catch me, strip off my clothes in front of everyone. They'd hold me down on one of the tables, feel me, handle me, touch my tits, my arse, finger my cunt. I wouldn't be able to stop them. They'd hold me down tight, stretched out over the table with everyone looking on . . .'

'Yes . . .' Fraser said, both his hands gripping the edge of the table, his whole body locked in anticipation of what she was going to make him do.

'I wouldn't be able to stop them. They'd open me up. Then the man would come in. The one I'd been running away from. See that table of men over there?'

He nodded, as though in a trance.

'I'd be on that table, all the plates and crockery and glass shattering around me. Then the man who'd been chasing me would take his cock out. Not even bother to undress, just take his cock out . . .'

'Yes . . .'

She felt his cock pulsing under the black silk. Using the circle of her thumb and forefinger she wanked it once more and immediately felt the wetness of his hot spunk shooting out into the veil of her knickers. . . 'And fuck me,' she said quietly, unnecessarily.

'Oh . . .' Fraser moaned loudly, emptying his lungs of breath. His body went limp, his eyes closed. The table of men heard the noise. As one, they turned to see where it had come from and what had caused it. Diana smiled angelically.

She caught the waiter's eye. It was not difficult. He was staring right at her. He hurried over.

'Can I have another napkin, please?' Diana said, smiling a winning smile.

'*Bien sûr.*'

He dashed off, his suspicions no doubt confirmed. Diana could feel Fraser's penis shrinking away. The waiter returned with an unstarched napkin and handed it to her.

'Everything is all right?'

'Perfectly,' Fraser said, regaining his composure.

The waiter shrugged his shoulders and departed. Diana used the napkin to wipe her hand dry then wrapped her knickers in the white linen and put it in her handbag. They could add it to Fraser's bill if they were so inclined.

'How did you know?'

'Know what?'

83

'It was so perfect, I mean your imagination. Everything. Exactly what I wanted.'

'I told you, I like it. I have an instinct. I don't know what it is . . .'

'I'd like to make this a regular date.'

'So would I.'

'Really?'

'Of course, Ronnie, you're a very attractive man. I'll arrange it with Carolyn.'

'Good.'

'I've just realised something.'

'What's that?'

'I don't know your name.'

'Ask for Kirsty.'

'Kirsty. I certainly wouldn't forget that.'

Diana finished the rest of her oysters and was hungry for her Dover sole. Fraser appeared to have lost his appetite.

The experience with Ronald Fraser had left Diana Wilson restless. They had talked amicably enough over the rest of the lunch and Fraser had been polite and attentive but clearly he was drained. By three o'clock he made his excuses and left.

Of course, what she felt more than anything was randy. The story she had made up for Fraser's benefit had turned her on too. The restaurant had called her a taxi. Fortunately the taxi-driver was old and fat. If he had been young and fit he might have got more than just the money for his fare.

In the past Diana had gone weeks, no, months, without sex. As Charles had never made any demands on her once the initial lust of their relationship waned, she seemed to have stopped thinking about sex altogether. Occasionally, spurred on by something she had seen on television, or some hunk of a man on the street, she'd attempted to masturbate. But it was hardly a success and getting little satisfaction from it did not encourage her to more frequent attempts. As her aerobics instructor had once said of muscles, 'if you don't use it, you lose it.' It was obviously the same with sex.

But now the opposite applied. Since embarking on her adventure, since The Event in the Portland Square Hotel, Diana seemed to have an endless appetite for sex. Considering the events of yesterday – day and night and morning – she could hardly say that she was suffering from sexual deprivation. But, after her experience with Fraser, she felt desperate – desperate was not too strong a word – desperate for cock. Perhaps, she thought, that was the difference between professional girls and amateurs like her. Perhaps a professional could have dealt with Fraser and felt nothing, treated it like a job of work. But Diana could not. It had affected her, made her body churn, made her excited. She was definitely an amateur.

The phone was ringing as she put the key in the front door. She managed to get to it before the ringing stopped.

'Yes?' she said a little breathlessly.

'Ms Wilson?'

'Yes.'

'It's Giles Foster.'

'Oh, hello,' she said. It was the estate agent. Before she had gone out this morning she had put in an offer for John Borland's house. It was well below the asking price.

'I'm pleased to tell you Mr Borland has accepted your offer.'

'Oh, that's great news.'

'He asked me to tell you as soon as possible.'

'That's very nice of him.'

'So, I've got your solicitor's address. Shall I ask them to contact his?'

'I had better do that, I suppose. Have you got the address?' She copied down the name and address.

'Do you need any help with mortgage arrangements?'

'No. I'll be taking care of that myself.'

'Well, you've bought yourself a house.'

'It appears so.'

Diana put the phone down and grinned. She was delighted. She hadn't expected Borland to accept such a low offer but he had. It was a new house and a new start.

The phone rang again while she was retrieving her keys from the front door.

'Hello?'

'Diana?' She recognised his voice immediately. It sounded even deeper and richer over the phone.

'John?'

'Foster's spoken to you.' It was not a question.

'How did you know that?'

'I got him to call me. Poor lad's been trying for hours.'

'I've been out.'

'Apparently. Are you in now?'

'In?'

'At home. Would you like a visitor?'

Diana could not think of anyone she would rather see. 'Oh, yes. Where are you?'

'In my car, parked in the road outside your house. I bribed Foster to give me the address. I thought we should celebrate your new purchase . . .'

'Come in, for God's sake.'

She put the phone down. Her heart was beating thirteen to the dozen and she felt breathless. The prospect of having her needs so quickly met made her feel almost dizzy with anticipation. She barely had time to unpin her hair and brush it out before the doorbell rang.

As she opened the door and saw Borland, she felt herself melting inside. He was more attractive than she remembered; rugged, strong, masculine. He was wearing green corduroy trousers, a rollneck blue sweater and a blue cardigan with a thick lapel like a jacket. He held a bottle of champagne in his hand.

'John . . . it's so good to see . . .'

She couldn't be bothered to finish the sentence. His mouth was just too kissable. She flung herself into his arms. He picked her up off her feet and kissed her.

The kiss lasted a long time. She could feel his erection swelling against her. All the time he held her aloft, her feet inches from the ground, his arms wrapped around her waist.

'I want you so much,' she said as he finally lowered her to the ground.

'Yes.' He said.

She fought with his belt in her hurry to get it unfastened. She just wanted to get at his cock. She couldn't think of anything else. His zip sang as she pulled it down, she had his belt unbuckled at last and the button on his trousers undone. She tugged his trousers and pants down over his arse.

'What's the rush . . .? There's plenty of time.'

She kissed him again. Somehow, she was not at all sure how, she forced him down until they were on the hall floor, lying together just inside the front door. The bottle of champagne lay on its side too.

'I need you,' she said stating what must have been obvious to him by now. She slid on to her back. She could feel the bristles of the doormat on the back of her calves. 'Fuck me . . .'

His hand went up under her skirt. With her knickers balled up in her handbag her cunt was exposed. It felt damp. He pulled her skirt up to her waist and mounted her. His cock slipped into her cunt like the piston in some well-oiled machine. She was wet. Soaking wet

He started to thrust into her, not understanding her urgency but catching it, being affected by it, suddenly needing her as much as she evidently needed him. Her need created his.

He felt her hands moving down to his buttocks, the only part of him that was naked. Her fingers dug in, urging him forward. He hardly needed any encouragement. His cock was rigid as it ploughed back and forth, his trousers round his knees, his naked arse bobbing in the air, her legs raised now, at either side of him, raised and bent. Her foot was against the hall table.

Diana had come the moment he had penetrated her, the moment his cock had slid effortlessly into her liquid cunt. Her whole body trembled and she gasped. It was easy, so easy. Her eyes closed. In her orgasm, in the blackness of it, she saw the waiter's eyes, the curiosity replaced by certainty;

she felt again that hot wet spunk seeping over her hand through the black silky knickers. She came, as she had wanted to come in the restaurant, men's eyes looking at her, devouring her, watching her come . . .

But that orgasm was like the first crack in a dam. He had fucked away her frustration but it was such a wonderful relief, the sheer pleasure made her want to come again, come for him this time, come over him.

She bucked her hips to meet his movement. Her foot sent the hall table flying. The phone fell to the floor. They were in a frenzy of motion. Neither cared for the other, the wanting was too urgent. They cared only for their own pleasure, to get their own satisfaction. But that increased the other's need. Like fed on like. It was desperate, imperative. The world was reduced to frantic striving. They were both gasping, moaning, screaming.

Diana felt his cock tense and knew he was going to come. Somewhere she could hear a female voice telling her to please hang up and dial again. Then she felt her eyes roll back in their sockets and she was gone, plunged into a long tunnel of shocking, crushing sensation, unable to feel anything, or so she thought. But then, deep inside her, she felt the jets of red-hot spunk lashing out of his cock. Her body heaved, her nerves, every nerve, kicked in to join the harmonics that vibrated her, propelling her further, longer, deeper. Time stopped. Place vanished. She felt herself suspended in a void, her body cut off from its senses, feeling instead only the huge waves of ecstacy to which it was prey.

The prickle of the doormat on her calves was the

first sensation she became aware of. Apparently she had lowered her legs back on to the floor and now the doormat's bristles bit through her stockings into her legs. Her stockings were laddered. She was still wearing her shoes.

John Borland rolled off her on to his side.

'You must have needed that.'

'Oh, I did,' she said. 'I've been thinking of you.' It wasn't exactly a lie. It was a half-truth.

'I'm flattered then.'

'You should be.'

Very unsteadily she got to her feet. She pulled the hall table back into position and replaced the phone. She hoped he wouldn't ask her what had happened to her knickers. He didn't.

'Would you like some of this champagne?'

Borland was sweating. That amount of physical effort while wearing two thick sweaters by the hall radiator had produced beads of sweat on his forehead.

'Come into the kitchen,' she said.

She lead the way, vaguely brushing her long hair with her fingers and pulling down her skirt. From the fridge she took a bottle of Perrier and poured them both a glass. He drunk it eagerly.

'We'll have the champagne in a minute.'

'I need a shower,' he said, peeling off his cardigan.

'We'll have the champagne in the bath,' she said.

Twenty minutes later they were naked and lying together in a hot steamy bath, champagne glasses in their hands. They were facing each other, Diana's feet either side of John's thighs. Her pendulous breasts seemed to float in the soapy water.

Diana moved her foot under John's thigh and massaged his balls and cock with her toes. He moved his foot too until he could feel her labia with his big toe. They both heard the front door open and close.

'Who's that?' John asked, slightly alarmed.

'Oh . . . it's my lodger.' Diana replied. It was practically true. Charles would go straight to his room to await his instructions. That was what he had been told to do every evening. And he was very obedient.

'Would you like to go to dinner tonight to celebrate?' John asked, apparently satisfied with her explanation.

'Celebrate what?'

'You've just bought a new house at a bargain price, remember?'

She had forgotten. Sex had driven everything else out of her head. 'Of course, yes . . . I'd love to.'

'I should have made you pay more.'

'Why didn't you?'

'Because I really wanted to sell before I left the country.'

'You're leaving?'

'My company's bought a brewery in Texas. I'm going over to supervise. I'll be back here a lot but it's for two years maybe three. I thought I'd start again when I finally returned to England.'

'You'll be back regularly?'

'Sure. At least once a month.'

'Well, that's something.'

'Of course, you affected my decision too.'

'Little me?' she said in mock surprise.

His big toe had started to insinuate itself between her nether lips.

'I wanted to sell to someone I liked.'

'Very sentimental.'

'That's how I am.'

She could feel his toe probing her sex. Curiously, the water had a drying effect, washing away her body's efforts to make her wet.

'There's something I'd like to do before dinner.'

'I hope it's the same thing I have in mind,' he said.

She felt his cock swelling. 'It is. Definitely.'

Diana picked up the sponge and sat up. She washed the soap off her breasts. Her nipples were hard.

'What about your lodger?'

'What about him?'

'You're not . . . we're not exactly quiet.'

Diana stood up. Water cascaded off her body. Her pubic hair was matted. It had formed itself into a sharp point from which water ran off. It looked almost as if she was peeing.

'It'll give him a thrill then, won't it? Poor chap doesn't get much excitement.' The idea of Charles listening to her make love excited her. 'I want you,' she said and meant it just as much as she had no more than thirty minutes before.

Chapter Four

It had been a busy week. She had seen her solicitor, made an appointment with her bank manager and arranged for the house to be surveyed.

The news that John Borland was about to leave the country had depressed her at first but, if she was absolutely honest with herself, it had not caused her too much concern. She was definitely not in the market for a long-term relationship with any man at the moment. She had only just discovered her freedom and had no intention of throwing it away again so soon. In fact the idea that she would see him once or twice a month had, after consideration, seemed an ideal arrangement.

There had been three appointments for Carolyn and she was now on her way to the fourth. As the address she had been given was in the suburbs and there were unlikely to be parking problems, she was driving herself. Indeed she managed to park almost outside.

She was fifteen minutes early. She sat in her car and made a list of things she needed to buy on the way home for the dinner she had planned with Ann that night. As soon as the digital clock on the dashboard of the Ford Granada clicked on to 4.00

she had got out of the car and walked up to the house.

The house was semi-detached but large, built before the Second World War, with a small driveway surrounded by a thick hedge. The art-deco bay window, and all the other windows of the house, were hung with net curtains.

Diana rang the doorbell. Much to her surprise it was opened by a woman.

'Oh . . . this is 26 Rushden Drive?'

'That's it. Come in, come in. You're expected.'

The woman was in her forties with a neat, rather old-fashioned, perm in hair that looked as though it had been dyed brunette. She was dumpy and overweight. The plain black skirt she wore appeared to be stretched over a substantial girdle. Her blouse was fluffy and pink, not the same shade of pink as her lamb's-wool slippers.

'This way, dear . . .' she said, closing the door after Diana and leading the way upstairs. The staircase was straight and steep, carpeted in a flowery pattern of orange and green. Maggie had not told her to expect a woman and Diana was puzzled.

'I used to do it myself, of course. Before we came into the money. We won the pools you know . . .' the woman was saying while Diana tried to remember what Maggie had said, 'not a big win but quite enough. Then I thought it's more fun for him with a nice young girl like yourself. Well, it's his only interest. And it doesn't do any harm, does it? Once in a while. I'm not that interested any more myself . . . I'll let you get on with it if you don't mind. I've got a load of washing in. I watch sometimes.'

They had arrived at the end of the corridor. 'It's

that door, dear,' the woman said. She took four fifty-pound notes from her skirt pocket. They were hot and crumpled. She handed them to Diana without a word and headed back downstairs.

Diana wasn't sure whether to knock or go straight in. She decided to knock. As there was no reply she turned the handle and opened the door. Inside, the room was warm, very warm, an almost tropical heat. It was furnished like any other bedroom except that the double bed was stripped and covered with a green rubber sheet. The curtains on the windows were drawn and the light, quite a bright light, came from the two bedside lamps.

Sitting in a small armchair was a small, thin man wearing spectacles. He was almost completely bald apart from a horseshoe of hair that ran round his head like a laurel wreath. His hair had been dyed from the same bottle as his wife used. His round, piggy eyes stared at Diana as she closed the door behind her. Despite the heat he was fully dressed in a grey suit, a sleeveless blue jumper and a shirt and tie.

'Your name is?' he said in a thin, high voice with a faint Scottish accent.

'Kirsty. And you're Mr MacDonald.'

'That is correct.'

'Well, Mr MacDonald. What can I do for you?'

'Would you take your things off and lie down on the bed, please. On your back on the bed.' He spoke precisely, as if he were ordering a meal, or dealing with a grocer.

He sat with his hands together in front of his face, the tips of his fingers touching his chin, as though he were praying.

Diana was wearing a cream-coloured dress that

had large gold buttons down the front. She began
to undo the top button.

'No,' he said immediately. 'Behind the screen if
you please.'

There was a small three-panelled wooden screen
in the corner of the room by the bed.

'Do you want me to take everything off?' she
asked.

'Completely nude, if you'd be so kind. It's better
that way.'

Stepping behind the screen Diana quickly stripped off her dress and the cream silk bra, suspender
belt and panties. This, she told herself, was not
going to be one of her more exciting experiences.
She had not the faintest stirring of arousal. It was
unusual for her. She rolled the white stockings off
her legs and stepped out of her shoes. Obediently
she came out from behind the screen and lay on
the bed. The rubber sheet felt cold and clammy
but the room was so warm the chill was welcome.
The distinct aroma of rubber, sweet and sickly,
made her immediately think of hospitals, though
she was not entirely sure why.

MacDonald stood up and came over to the bed.

'A fine-looking woman. A fine-looking woman ... '
he said to himself. 'Please open your legs.'

Diana obeyed. MacDonald stared into the thick
pubic hair that veiled her sex.

'I have to examine you.'

'Like a doctor?' Diana asked.

'Exactly like a doctor,' he said enthusiastically.

His eyes were riveted on her labia, and she saw
a bulge developing in the front of his trousers.

'Does it hurt?'

'Hurt?'

'Is it painful?'

'Oh . . .' she realised what he wanted her to say, the role he wanted her to play. 'Yes.'

'Where does it hurt? Can you show me exactly?'

Diana ran her hand down into her pubic hair and parted it to expose her pink flesh. 'Here,' she said. 'And here.' She moved her finger along her sex and up to her clitoris.

'When does it hurt?'

'When?'

'All the time or just when you're having sexual intercourse?'

'When I'm being fucked . . .'

'When a penis is inserted?'

'Yes, doctor. That's it exactly. Can you help me?' Diana asked. She knew what the game was now. The bulge in his trousers was firm.

'I can. I have an ointment that I can prescribe.'

'Will it help?'

'Yes. Definitely. I will give you the first application myself.'

'Oh, I would appreciate that, doctor.'

'Very well then.'

From the pocket of his jacket he took a tube of KY jelly. From the other pocket he took a pair of rubber surgical gloves. 'You understand I would not normally do this . . .' he said solemnly. 'But as you are in such pain . . .'

'Oh, I am. It's very kind of you, doctor.'

He eased his rather porky fingers into the rubber then unscrewed the cap of the tube. He squeezed a little of the colourless gel on to the tip of his finger. 'You must tell me exactly where it hurts.'

He leant over her. His fingertip touched her labia. Diana felt the cold, wet cream.

'Here?' he asked.

'Higher up, doctor,' she said. His finger found her clitoris.

'Here?'

'Yes.'

'It's swollen.'

'Yes.'

He massaged her clitoris lightly. Diana felt a little shock of excitement. She could see his eyes locked on to her sex.

'Only here?'

'And inside. Right inside.'

He took his hand away, squeezed a great gob of jelly on to his fingers and put it back on her sex. He found the entrance to her cunt and inserted a finger into it. Another soon followed. The jelly made her wet. A third finger went back to her clitoris. The smell of the rubber and the jelly filled her nostrils. He had a soft touch.

'That feels so much better, doctor.'

'Does it?' His other hand unzipped his fly and felt inside for his cock. He did not extract it however, merely rubbing it up and down against his belly.

'You've got such strong hands,' she said.

'Doctor's hands . . .' he said, almost to himself.

'Yes, doctor's hands.'

What he was doing to her was extremely pleasant. It was not making her come but it was a delicious sensation. Diana bent one of her legs at the knee. She would have liked him to stroke her breasts too . . .

The bedroom door opened and Mrs MacDonald came in. She came to stand with her husband at the foot of the bed, her eyes looking down at Diana's sex as her husband's hand manipulated it gently.

'Oh, she's a very pretty one, isn't she, Dougie?' she said in a whisper. She had an expression on her face like an indulgent mother watching her son doing his homework.

'She's been in a great deal of pain,' he said. 'But this'll make it better.'

'Oh, yes. You're good at that. You made me better didn't you?'

'Oh ...' his voice wavered. His body tensed and Diana could feel the fingers inside her go rigid.

'Come on, Dougie ...' his wife said.

'Oh ... oh ...'

'Look at her.'

The hand in his fly stopped moving. He uttered a final low throaty moan, almost like a sob, and rocked forward against the bed, his eyes closed. A dark wet stain spread across his underpants.

After a few minutes, with his eyes still closed, he withdrew his fingers from Diana's body.

'Oh, that feels so much better,' she said, feeling that the little play should at least have a closing line.

'Good. Please get dressed behind the screen.'

Five minutes later Diana was dressed and sitting behind the steering wheel of her car. As she started the engine the digital clock clicked on to read 4.20. She had earned £10 per minute.

'And that was all he did?' Ann asked.

'That's all. I think it was the most peculiar so
far. And his wife popping in as if all he was doing
was playing with his train set.'

'Playing doctors and nurses . . .'

'Exactly. It just makes you wonder how on earth
he got hooked on that.'

'Maybe he was in hospital for a long time . . .'

'Then you'd think he'd want you to play a nurse.'

'God knows . . .'

They were having dinner in Diana's dining room.
Both women were casually dressed, Diana in a leotard and leggings in a leopard-skin print and Ann
in a baggy white Aran sweater and black slacks.
They had eaten casually too, a bowl of home-made
soup, baguettes, a green salad and three or four
different cheeses.

'Do you still, find it exciting?' Ann asked, cutting
herself another finger of Reblochon.

'Yes . . .' Diana said. 'Even this afternoon . . .'

'You found that exciting?'

'No, of course not. Not at the time. He had a nice
touch. But now, in retrospect. I can see myself lying
on that rubber sheet. I can see his eyes looking at
me. I can feel those sticky fingers . . .' She stopped
and looked at her friend. Their eyes met and Diana
felt herself shiver, a shiver of pleasure. 'Do you
want some fruit?' She handed Ann the large fruit
bowl with grapes, pears, oranges and apples.

Ann took some grapes. 'You always get the kinky
ones. I only get straights. Not that I'm
complaining.'

'It's Maggie. She thinks I can cope.'

'You can.'

'What about you?'

'What about me?'

'Do you still find it exciting?'

'Honestly?'

'Ann . . .'

'Honestly I don't think I've ever had such a good time in my life. I've been taken to some wonderful restaurants – you know how much I love food . . .' As if to demonstrate the point she took a pear from the fruit bowl and quartered it with a knife. '. . . And had unlimited sex. Even the sex that wasn't that good was tolerable. On top of which, entirely incidentally, I've got paid five times what I was earning working for fatso Malcolm. And . . .'

'And?' Diana prompted.

'There's you. Us, I mean. If you hadn't started all this we'd never have done anything, would we?'

'Necessity is the mother of invention.'

'Right. And speaking personally I'm very glad we did.'

'Oh, so am I.' Diana took her friend's hand. 'Talking of which, you are staying the night?'

'What about Charles?'

'What about him?'

'We can be awfully noisy.'

'You're the second person who's pointed that out.'

'Am I?'

'John . . .'

'Of course. You had him here?'

'Had being the operative word. With Charles in his bedroom.'

'And he didn't say anything.'

'If he had he wouldn't be living here any more, Ann. It's as simple as that.'

'He just takes it?'

'Apparently. Washes, cleans, scrubs. Talking of which let's go through into the living room. He can make us some coffee.'

They got up and walked into the living room. Charles was sitting in an armchair reading a newspaper. He sprang to his feet and folded the paper neatly, the moment they came through the door.

'Coffee.' Diana ordered. 'And clean up the dining room. We're finished.'

Without a word, Charles scurried out of the room. Ann started to laugh.

'Come and sit here,' Diana said, sitting on the sofa. As soon as Ann sat down Diana kissed her full on the mouth, feeling the softness of her lips that had given her so much pleasure in the past weeks. Her hand found Ann's breast under the sweater and squeezed gently. The kiss lasted a long time.

'I'm feeling so sexy,' she said, pulling away from the kiss.

'You make me feel sexy,' Ann replied. 'Every time is like the first. I don't think I've ever been so excited in my life.'

Ann repositioned herself on the sofa with her hand in Diana's lap.

'Scared and excited.'

'Yes. Scared at first.'

There was a timid knock on the door.

'Come,' Diana called.

Charles came in carrying a tray of coffee and a plate of marzipan petits fours. He put the tray on the table in front of the sofa, his eyes not looking at either of the women.

Ann had never liked Charles. So much so that she had advised her friend not to marry him. When the marriage had proved a disaster Ann had been careful not to say, 'I told you so.'

'So, Diana tells me you're a new man, Charles,' Ann said. 'Now she's discovered your secrets. You've certainly lost a bit of weight.'

Charles said nothing.

'He has, hasn't he? A lot more to lose yet though.' Diana added.

'Your wife is a very beautiful woman? Don't you think so?' Ann felt coquettish. She caressed Diana's cheek then kissed her on the mouth pressing her body against hers, kissing with her eyes open so she could see the expression on Charles' face. She wanted to test him. It was exciting. She felt her heartbeat increase.

'Well, Charles? Answer Ann's question?' Diana said sternly.

'Very,' he said and clearly meant it.

'Go.' Diana ordered.

Charles vanished immediately obviously glad to have been dismissed and escape further teasing.

They drank coffee and talked about their experiences over the last weeks. The noise of dishes being cleared away next door assured Diana that Charles was doing his duty. After a while she heard him go upstairs and his bedroom door close.

'Come one,' Diana said. 'Let's go to bed.'

She stood up and took her friend's hand.

As soon as they were in the bedroom they kissed, standing together pressing themselves into each other, their arms interlaced around their bodies, Diana's head tilted back by Ann's height. Not a

103

word was said. Diana took Ann's sweater and pulled it over her head. She could see the excitement in her eyes and knew it reflected her own.

Ann was not wearing a bra. She unzipped the slacks herself and let them fall to the floor. Her black knickers soon followed them. She stood naked, her legs slightly apart. Her pubic hair was so sparse – as though it had been shaved and only grown back recently – it hid nothing. Diana could see the beginning of the gash of her sex.

Sitting on the bed, Diana pulled her leggings off. As soon as they were clear Ann dropped to her knees in front of Diana pulling her legs apart, insinuating her body between them until her naked tits were hard against Diana's navel. She tilted her head back, her turn now, and they kissed. Diana ran her fingers through Ann's short black hair, squeezing Ann's body between her legs.

Ann's mouth broke the kiss. She kissed Diana's throat and neck, her bare arms, her breasts under the leotard, and her belly. Her fingers found the three press-studs that held the crotch of the leotard in place and worked them free, glorying in the feeling of Diana's soft labia underneath. The leotard sprang open.

At once, Ann sunk her mouth on to Diana's sex. It was hot. She pushed her tongue through the mat of hair as Diana pulled the leotard over her head. The tongue found its target, the pink bud of clitoris, and lapped at it as though tasting some delicious exotic fruit.

'Oh . . .' Diana gasped, only too aware that her husband would be listening in his bedroom. Did she gasp louder than usual?

Ann's tongue was perfect. The perfect pressure. The perfect rhythm. The perfect place. Diana let herself fall back on to the bed. She closed her eyes. Her mind filled with images, her body with feeling. Memories. Snapshots like a photograph album flicked through at random. The little bald man's hand working in his trousers, the twins intertwined together, John Borland's hard muscular body fucking her in front of a log fire.

She wanted to touch and caress Ann, to do to Ann what she was doing to her, but it was too late, her orgasm was too close. All she could do was lay on the bed and moan, tossing her head from side to side, moaning louder and louder as Ann's mouth wrung feelings out of her that were simply exquisite. She felt Ann's fingers at the entrance to her cunt, and knew she would plunge them into her, deep and hard, as soon as she felt her orgasm, so as to make it longer, driving her higher. She loved that.

Ann felt her friend's body. She knew it so well now, all the tell-tale signs, the different noises Diana made, her voice changing from the expression of pleasure to the stating of desperate need. As she felt her orgasm trembling on the edges of her body she thrust her fingers deep into the wet silky walls of her cunt.

Diana came. She came over Ann's mouth and fingers. She came sharply, intensely, almost painfully, her body twisting into a knot of ecstasy, her eyes rolled back, every nerve focused on her cunt. The orgasm made her scream not moan. It was slow to leave her body. Ann's fingers probed it, poked it, provoked it into little shocks that made Diana's body arch and tense all over again.

'I want to see you,' Diana said, regaining the power to form meaningful words rather than inarticulate sounds.

Ann got to her feet unself-consciously. She stood by the bed and allowed Diana to look at her. Her breasts were not large but firm and round. Though her body was big she was not fat and it was well-proportioned. Her neck was long and sinewy, her waist well-defined, her navel not as flat as Diana's but not bulging either, and below the thin gauzy pubic hair her long legs looked strong and powerful. In another life, Diana thought, Ann would have been a Warrior Queen.

'You're beautiful,' Diana said simply.

'I'm glad you think so.'

'Please . . .' Diana pulled herself back into the middle of the bed and patted the sheet next to her.

Ann knelt beside Diana and reached out to touch her breasts. Gravity had thrown them to either side of her chest. Ann gathered them up, kneading the soft flesh and feeling a flush of passion as she did so. But, if she were honest with herself, she was not thinking of Diana now, but of herself. This was for her pleasure. She felt her body respond, her sex pulsing. She realised, quite unexpectedly, that she was thinking of Charles.

Diana pulled Ann down beside her. She kissed her mouth and tasted her own juices on Ann's lips. Her mouth slipped down to Ann's neck, licking and sucking, taking tiny, playful bites of flesh between her teeth, reaching for her breasts and doing the same there, then sucking in her nipple and pinching it between her teeth until she heard Ann gasp with pleasure.

Lower, she licked her way down to Ann's navel, probing her belly button with her tongue. She saw Ann opening her legs. Her mouth descended further, into the little wisps of hair, down to the runnel of Ann's sex.

Ann arched her hips off the bed, her legs apart, her knees bent, her heels digging into the sheets.

Diana's hot tongue slid on to her sex and Ann moaned. She could feel Diana's heavy breasts trailing across her navel as the tip of her tongue found her pink clitoris and tapped it like a tiny soft hammer. Ann's sex was wet. It had been wet since she had seen Charles, since she had teased him, since the idea, coming from where she did not know, had occurred to her that she would really like to tease him more. As Diana tongued between her legs, long full licks punctuated by little darting penetrations of her cunt and hard prodding of her clitoris Ann felt her orgasm begin to swell through her body.

She saw the look in Charles' eye as she had kissed his wife. She had seen the expression on his face. His acceptance, his subservience. It had thrilled her. She didn't know how or why but it had touched her sexual psyche. It had made her feel wild. It had created something in her, or stirred something that was already there but buried, buried so deep it had never been roused before.

She wished Charles was here now, watching. She wanted to see that look again.

In her mind he walked into the room, stood at

the foot of the bed, looked down at them . . .

'Oh, my God . . .' Her orgasm took her completely
by surprise. It was so sudden, so strong, so completely out of control. One moment her body was
throbbing quietly, the next it had exploded. Diana
had barely started a rhythm. Ann's body shook violently her thighs involuntarily squeezing Diana's
head.

It was a long time before Ann's body relaxed
again. Diana drew her head away slowly.

'Anyone would think you were sex-starved . . .'
Diana said, lying down beside her friend and stroking her arm.

'Yes . . . It was so strong. I was . . .' Ann hesitated.
They had always been truthful with each other. But
she wasn't sure about this truth.

'You were what?'

'I just got this funny idea . . . image . . .'

'What?'

'You'll think I'm getting kinky . . .'

'Come on . . .'

'Of Charles watching us . . .'

'Charles!'

'Yes. There was something in the way he looked
when I kissed you downstairs. It turned me on.
Don't ask me why.'

'Really?'

'That's what made me come so quickly.'

'Domina was right then.'

'Domina?'

'Don't you remember? When we met her at the
party. She said you were a natural.'

'I'd forgotten.'

'Well?'

'Well, what?'

'Do you want to do it?'

'What?'

'Have Charles watch?'

A shiver ran through Ann's body, like an orgasm in miniature. 'You're joking.' She tried to sound calm.

'Why not? He should be so lucky.'

Ann felt another jolt of passion.

Diana got up off the bed.

'We can't,' Ann said.

'We can,' Diana replied quietly.

Charles must have heard their activities. His whole sexuality was directed to submission. Diana had no qualms about letting him see a woman giving her the pleasure he had never wanted to give her. She had no qualms about using him in any way at all. If he didn't like it he could go. It was as simple as that. She went over to the wastebin by the chest of drawers and picked out the white stockings she had worn today. They had laddered as she put them back on behind MacDonald's little screen.

Without bothering to put on a robe Diana walked down to Charles' room and opened the door. Charles was lying on the thin mattress in the bare room, naked. He was caught by surprise. His erection, red and hard, was sticking out of the top of his fist. He snatched his hand away.

'Stand up,' Diana ordered. She was doing this for Ann but that did not mean she didn't feel her own excitement. Her body was still full of the pleasure of sex, visions of Ann's body and her own intertwined. Feelings Ann had created in her still rumbled around inside, like thunder on a hot stormy night, occasionally breaking into a loud deep clap long after the main storm had passed, never quite going away.

It was not the moment now, but if she decided to keep Charles she made a mental note that she was going to have to find a way to stop him masturbating whenever he chose. That was definitely not a privilege he should be allowed.

Charles got to his feet, his erection sticking out in front of him not at all diminished by the sudden intrusion.

'Put your hands behind your back.'

He obeyed meekly. Diana looped one of the stockings around his wrists and inexpertly, but effectively, bound them together. She balled up the other stocking and stuffed it into his mouth.

'Now follow me.'

Diana walked back into her bedroom with Charles following her. She knew his eyes would be feasting on her long legs and pouting arse.

Ann was lying on the bed, her legs open, her knees bent, both her hands playing aggressively with her own sex.

'You look so turned on . . .' Diana said stating the obvious. Ann's face was flushed.

'I am . . .' Ann replied. 'I couldn't stop myself. Just the thought . . .' She stopped as Charles shuffled into the room.

'Wouldn't it be better if I did that?'

Diana climbed on to the bed. From the drawer in the bedside table she took a large cream-coloured dildo.

'Oh, yes . . .' Ann said her eyes looking at Charles' face as he watched the two naked bodies on the bed. His expression was the same as it had been downstairs, a mixture of need and lust and hopelessness. It thrilled her again. She opened her legs wider, angling her cunt at him, as if to taunt him with it.

Kneeling at her side, Diana caressed the curve of Ann's pubic bone with her hand, teasing her clitoris, then leaving it alone. She had never felt her friend so wet. Her juices seemed to be running out of her as though someone had turned on a tap. With her other hand she positioned the dildo at the entrance to her cunt, nudging aside the thick labia.

'Yes, yes . . . Do it.' Ann begged as she felt the cold, hard head of the dildo probing her body. Her eyes had not left Charles. She wanted him to see everything, wanted him to see her fucked by the inanimate plastic while his own cock ached for release.

Diana thrust the dildo home, arching it into Ann's body. Ann gasped then pushed herself down on to it and began bucking her hips, letting Diana know the rhythm she wanted. Diana's fingertip was on her clitoris as the dildo slid in and out, immediately slicked with Ann's copious juices.

Charles watched. He had never seen such a sight. In all the years he had paid Domina to use and abuse him, it had never been like this. He needed to wank so badly, his cock throbbed and ached, as hard as steel. But his hands were tied. All he could do was watch. All he could do was submit. Their will was stronger than his. He saw Ann's eyes, saw how they looked at him, saw how they appeared to relish his submission.

Ann was moaning with every inward thrust. It

was almost the word 'yes' but not quite. She repeated it over and over again. She was coming. She was coming violently, completely out of control. The dildo filled her, every inch of her, the tip of Diana's finger unerringly working exactly the right spot on her clitoris at the same time.

But it wasn't the physical situation that was making her come. As her body begun to shudder, as her orgasm rattled every nerve, every muscle, every sinew in her body, she came finally, unable to keep her eyes open. It was the image of Charles that made her come, burnt into her mind like a brand. His eyes looking at her, his greedy, hungry, hopeless eyes, watching the dildo glistening with her juices, sliding in and out of her sex. In her mind he came closer and closer, bending forward to see every detail. It felt as if his eyes were boring into her, sending out hot rays of feeling, ploughing into her just as hard as the dildo.

Her body arched off the bed as though pulled by some invisible magnet hung above her, every muscle stretched and taut. Then she fell back exhausted, replete, a slack damp heap. Diana let the dildo slip from her cunt of its own accord.

She did not rest for long. She had other priorities and only allowed herself seconds of lying in the pool of delicious post-orgasmic sensation . . .

Ann was surprised when she opened her eyes to see that Charles had not moved, though his eyes were still locked to her body. She looked at Diana who was still kneeling, her big breasts topped by hard nipples, her legs apart, the thick fleece of her pubic hair damp and slightly flattened.

Kneeling up in front of her, Ann manoeuvred her

breasts until her nipples touched against Diana's. She moved them from side to side so they brushed together.

'Nice . . .' Diana said smiling at her friend.

'They feel so hard.'

'Like pebbles.'

Ann pushed her breasts forward until their bodies were pressed together and their breasts were squashed with the nipples, the hard stones of their nipples, crushed against their rib cages.

'Shall I use the dildo now?' Ann asked only too aware that Charles could hear.

'No . . .' Diana loved the feeling in her breasts, she closed her eyes and writhed her body against her friend. She could feel Ann's knees against her own, she could feel the thick bush of her pubic hair against Ann's pubis, she could feel her clitoris, swollen and throbbing, hanging down between her open legs like a tiny cock. 'Feel me . . .' she said.

Ann wrapped one arm around Diana's body while the other moved down between her legs. Her finger found Diana's clitoris. She pressed it, pressed it hard into the pubic bone. Diana moaned, her body jolted with pleasure.

Ann's finger circled the tiny bud of flesh. Her other hand dropped to Diana's bottom, cupping the cheek of her arse, pushing it forward to meet her own body. She moved rhythmically, as though fucking her friend with a cock, bucking her hips to and fro as her finger made delicate loops around the pink, swollen bud of nerves.

She could feel Diana's reaction. Pressed together as they were, thigh on thigh, breast on breast, she felt Diana's body quiver. It was like playing a musical instrument, producing music so sweet, so harmonic, so powerful it went straight to the source of emotion. She played Diana and felt the harmonies vibrating in her own body.

They kissed. Diana sucked on Ann's tongue, nibbled at her lips, wrapped one arm around Ann's back, another at her shoulder. She didn't want the kiss to end until she had her fill. Somewhere in her mind, at the back of her mind, she heard her voice telling Charles to watch, telling him this was the body he'd neglected all those years, this was what it was capable of, and this was his punishment, to watch her being pleasured beyond her wildest dreams.

She could feel herself coming, her body begin to churn, her passion focusing, every stroke of Ann's fingering bringing her closer and closer. Ann's hand on her bottom was moving down between the deep cleft of her buttocks, down until she felt it at her anus, then down between her labia.

Ann dipped her finger in the juices of Diana's cunt then, her finger lubricated, she positioned it at the puckered mouth of Diana's anus. As if to tell her she was right, that she wanted the penetration, Diana sucked harder on Ann's tongue. The message was received. Ann pushed her finger in, deep in, right up to her knuckle.

Diana saw her husband out of the corner of her eye. She saw the look on his face, a look of agony, of seeing so much sex, raw sex and knowing that, for him, it was forbidden fruit. Ann was not the only one turned on by his submission ...

'Oh, darling ... oh, Ann ...' Diana managed to cry as she felt Ann's finger exploring the tight pas-

sage of her arse, reaming into it, wanting to take
her over the edge by its intrusion. She succeeded.
Diana came, her orgasm ripping away her sense of
anything but the exploding, cascading ecstasy that
flooded her body. She clung to Ann's strong body
like a drowning man to a piece of flotsam, as her
body convulsed open and prey to every sensation.

It was a long time before her body had finished
with her. A long time before she was prepared to
release her friend, before the tremors and after-
shocks that raked through her, finally abandoned
their attempts to thrill her one final time.

They both sank back on to the bed and lay in
each other's arms. But, though her sexual energy
was spent, Diana had no thought of sleep. Since
Ann was so fascinated with her husband's new situation she wanted to give her one final demonstration of his capabilities. Or was she testing him
for herself, for her own pleasure?

'Go back to your room, Charles,' she ordered.

'My hands . . .' he managed to mumble through
his stocking gag.

'Now.'

Charles turned and walked out, his cock bobbing
up and down in front of him.

Diana got to her feet.

'What are you going to do?' Ann asked.

'Are you tired?'

'No.'

'Come on then.'

Diana pulled on a white satin robe that hung on
the back of the bedroom door. 'Do you want a
robe?'

'Where are we going?'

'We're going to give Charles a surprise.'

'I'm fine like this,' Ann said standing up. She put on her high heels. They increased her height dramatically.

Charles had managed to close his bedroom door. He couldn't turn out the overhead light however, with his hands still bound behind his back. He had assumed they had finished with him, his punishment over. He lay on the mattress on his stomach rubbing his cock against it. He had spat the stocking out and it lay in a wet ball by his head.

'Stop that,' Diana barked as she strode into the room for the second time that night. 'Get on to your back.'

He did as he was told. With his hands behind him his body was bowed up off the bed. His cock stood at right angles to his thighs.

'You're going to show Aunty Ann your party piece, though you don't deserve it . . .'

Diana had brought the riding crop in a smart shop just off Bond Street. It was identical to the one Domina had used on him.

'His party piece?' Ann said.

'Domina trained him. Didn't she?'

'Yes.'

'Yes what?'

'Yes, mistress.'

Ann's eyes widened as Diana explained. She handed Ann the whip. Experimentally Ann slashed it through the air once or twice. Charles' body cringed at each swipe.

'Will it really work?' Ann asked.

Diana smiled and nodded.

Ann stood over Charles, the power and strength

116

in her naked body all too clear. She held the whip
in her hand. She could see Charles eyeing it. She
touched the loop of leather to the tip of his cock
where a tear of fluid had formed. The leather sponged up the fluid, darkening the tan hide. Then she
flipped the whip back and slapped Charles' thigh a
stinging blow.

'One,' he said, like an automaton. This was his
training, this is what Domina had taught him in
their expensive lessons. But Domina could not com-
pare to this giant Amazon who towered over him
now, her eyes blazing with excitement.

Ann slashed again, this time higher up, nearer
his rampant cock.

'Two,' he intoned. He'd never make it to ten. He
looked at his wife, her body wrapped in white satin.
He looked up at Ann, her breasts trembling with
effort, the slit of her sex visible under her wispy
pubic hair.

The third blow was harder, across both thighs.

'Three,' he managed to say. But his whole body
was concentrated on his cock now. It felt as though
it would burn it was so hot. He would never
make it to ten, never hold on, not after all they
had put him through. He was too full of spunk, too
excited, too turned on . . .

Ann aimed the next blow, rising her arm high. It
hit his thigh half-an-inch from his erection.
Immediately his cock spasmed.

'Fo . . .' Spunk jetted into the air in a high arch,
spattering down on his body. A spot or two landed
on Ann's thigh. White hot spunk. Even when the
spectacular eruption had finished, spunk seeped
from the little oval gash in his glans.

117

'You see . . .' Diana said. 'Domina trained him
well, don't you think?'

Ann did not reply. She had seen it all now. She
had heard about it and read about it – domination
and submission, mistresses and slaves – but now
she had seen it, experienced it for herself. It had
affected her, affected her in a way she had never
dreamt of. She had fantasised about many things
but never this. Clearly this evening had tapped
deep into her psyche, stirred emotions she had no
idea she possessed.

Well, it appeared Domina had been right. Not
only was she a natural physically but mentally too.
The Warrior Queen. And she was certainly in a
position to exploit her feelings. With Charles of
course. And with other men.

She smiled to herself. In the morning she would
call Maggie at Carolyn's office. If they had clients
whose penchant was in this area of sexual endeav-
our Ann Connell was definitely the right person for
the job . . .

They slept heavily and dreamlessly. Charles
brought them breakfast in bed. Both women sat
up, their naked breasts for once not displaying
erect nipples. Their nipples slept on. Neither
woman made any effort to cover themselves.

Charles laid the tray down on the bed. He waited
for instructions, feeling his cock stirring. He
couldn't help but stare. He had hardly slept at
all.

'Get out, Charles,' Diana said. 'What are you
staring at? You've seen tits before.'

Had Charles hoped there would be more? Had

he hoped they would resume where they had left
off last night? He was enslaved now, totally. He
wanted only to be allowed to stay, to wait on his
wife. It was what he'd always wanted from a
woman. Last night had been a dream, like a long
animated dream.

'Go . . .' Diana barked again.

He trotted out obediently. All he wanted was to
obey.

Chapter Five

'So, I need a mortgage,' Diana said finishing her explanation about the house.

'I understand . . .' The bank manager was no more than thirty. His suit was cheap and the collar of his shirt was ever so slightly frayed. He wore a comparatively expensive watch but everything else about him spoke of being over-worked and poorly paid. He was not unattractive Diana thought. He was tall, with a mop of black curly hair, brown eyes and a fresh complexion that looked as though he played a lot of sport – cricket in the summer, rugby in the winter. 'The problem is . . .'

Diana had dressed deliberately. Her best black suit with its modest skirt cut just above the knee. A yellow blouse buttoned to the neck. No cleavage. No thighs. The image of a business woman . . .

'The problem is,' he repeated, 'your income.'

'My income?'

'Well, your account has been relatively inactive over the past years. But recently . . .' He consulted the papers in a buff file on his desk, flicking from one to another. 'Recently it has become extremely . . . er . . . busy.'

'So I have the income to support a mortgage.'

'Well now . . . I'm afraid it is not as easy as that. We have to look at the position over the long-term, over a period of years, not just a few months. Looked at like this, there is very little income . . .'

'But that's the past. My earnings will be considerable . . .'

'You see, how are we to know that? Look at it from our point of view. If you had so little income before, even as short a time as four months ago, what is to guarantee that it won't return to these levels in, say, another four months?'

'I see. I should have explained. I've started a business.'

'Ah . . .' He sat forward in his chair and picked his pen up. 'That puts an entirely different complexion on the matter . . .'

'Good.'

'I'd better take down some details.'

'Details?'

'Company name, or is it private? Some idea of your assets, your cash flow, your business plan. The nature of the business, of course. Your projections for growth. Then I'm sure we can look very favourably on your mortgage application especially if your account recently reflects the business's success.'

'Oh . . .'

'Is that a problem?'

'Oh, yes. I mean, no. No. It's just I didn't bring anything with me.'

'Well, that's fine. Why don't I make another appointment and you can bring in all the accounts. We'll need current cash flow and some sort of projection over the next two or three years. You're obviously doing very well. What sort of business is it actually?'

'Sorry?' Pretending she hadn't heard the question gave Diana time to think.

'What sort of business? Manufacturing, service industry?'

'Oh, service industry...'

'And what sort of service?'

'Well, I suppose you could say it was catering to people's fantasies...'

'Really?' He said appearing to be genuinely interested. 'What like special treats, parties, birthdays, that sort of thing?'

'Yes. Parties... whatever they've always dreamt of.'

'Fine, fine. Well, as I said, judging from your account it seems you have got off to a flying start. I'm sure if we take a projection based on these figures we can certainly get you the mortgage you require. Shall I say four pm tomorrow?'

'Yes, that'll be OK,' Diana said.

The manager got up from behind his desk. Diana stood up too.

'I must say it's been a pleasure to meet you at last, Ms Wilson. I've only been here three months. I haven't met all the customers yet.'

'A pleasure to meet you too.' Diana said.

He shook her hand and showed her out of his office to the main concourse of the bank.

'See you tomorrow then...'

Out on the street Diana was in a daze. She supposed she should have guessed that the bank wouldn't have given her a mortgage on such flimsy proof of income but it had never occurred to her.

123

She'd just assumed that with so much in her account they would have been only too happy to lend her more.

It was thoroughly depressing. She could hardly tell them the real source of her income. She couldn't invent a business overnight, produce accounts, invoices, orders . . .

Without a mortgage she couldn't buy John Borland's house, or any house for that matter. Her whole future plans would have to be abandoned.

Gloomily, she drove home. In her kitchen she made a cup of tea and sat drinking it at the kitchen table trying to think of some way to convince the bank to give her a mortgage.

The phone rang.

'Hello?'

'Diana, John.'

'Oh, hello,' she said. Heaven forbid he should read her thoughts.

'You sound depressed.'

'No, I'm fine.' She tried to make her voice more cheerful.

'Look, you know that friend you're always talking about.'

'Ann?'

'Yes, Ann. Do you think she'd like to come out to dinner with us. I've got a friend I'd like her to meet.'

'Is he nice?'

'He's lonely. It's his treat.'

'I'm sure she'd love to.'

'Tomorrow?'

'I'll have to check with her.'

'Of course. Ring me back could you? We'll come and pick you up if that's all right. Where do you fancy going?'

'Somewhere swish. Ann's very into food?'

'Le Gavroche, the Connaught Grill . . .'

'You are splashing out.'

'To tell you the truth my friend isn't short of a few shillings . . .'

'The Connaught then.'

'Good choice. They've got a claret I've always wanted to try. I'd have to mortgage my house to afford it.'

Diana almost choked.

'You coughing? Are you all right?'

'Just swallowed my breath,' she gasped.

'Tell you what, don't bother to ring unless there's a problem. We'll come and pick you up at eight.'

'Can't wait . . .'

Having to tell John Borland that she could not afford to buy his house, and that she'd been wasting his time, was not a scene she wanted to contemplate.

By six o'clock Diana felt thoroughly miserable. She had spent all afternoon trying to think of something to tell her bank manager and come up with precisely nothing. She had spoken to Ann on the phone to confirm their date but Ann could think of nothing either, though she promised to try. It looked as though she was going to change all her plans.

She'd asked Ann round, to take her mind of things but Ann was doing her exercise class that evening and then had a appointment for Carolyn. Diana had to do something. She didn't want to spend the evening alone fretting over her problems.

An idea struck her out of the blue. She couldn't

remember where she'd put the telephone number.
Months ago, at the beginning, only a few days after
The Event, when she hadn't even owned a suspender belt or a decent pair of knickers, she'd gone
to a lingerie shop in the High Street. In its changing room she had met a woman. The woman had
been odd, enigmatic, intriguing. She'd given Diana
her telephone number and told her to call. She had
spoken to her once and had been supposed to call
again. With all that had happened she'd forgotten.
Until now. She may have forgotten deliberately,
subconsciously. What the woman had said to her
had thrilled her, but in a strange way it had fright-
ened her too.

She found the number scribbled on the back of a
sales invoice from the lingerie shop. It was tucked
away in her handbag.

She dialled the number and quickly put the
phone down before it could ring out. She could hear
the woman's voice, hard and serious (I'm a lesbian
– that's what I do). She dialled the number a
second time and a second time put the phone down
before it could ring. Is this what she wanted?
Another new experience? With Ann, having sex
with another woman had been easy, comforting,
effortless. They had discovered it together. But this
woman was a stranger. ('It's different with a
stranger.')

Diana realised her heart was beating faster. She
could feel it pounding against her ribs.

She dialled again. The phone rang twice.

'Julie?' she said, when a woman's voice answered.

'Hello, Diana.'

'How did you know it was me?'

'I've been waiting for you to call.'

'I wondered . . .'

'You were supposed to ring me a couple of weeks ago . . .'

'I've been busy.'

'It doesn't matter. You're ringing now.'

'I wondered if you were busy tonight. Perhaps we could meet . . .'

'Come round here. I'll give you the address.'

Diana noted it down. 'About an hour.'

'An hour's fine, Diana.'

'See you later, then.'

'I'll be waiting, Diana.'

Diana put the phone down. Her heart was beating so fast now she could hear it. The receiver of the phone was wet. Her palms had been sweating.

It was not more than a twenty-minute drive. The house was large and detached standing in a garden that looked as though it needed a lot of attention. Nettles and weeds grew in what had once been neatly organised flower-beds. Diana parked outside and walked up the five tiled steps to the front door. The door needed work too. The paint was flaking off and one of the glass panes set in its panelling was cracked.

Diana had a strong urge to flee. It passed. She pressed the small brass doorbell and heard a ringing somewhere deep inside the house. The urge to flee returned. It increased as the seconds passed. She was about to turn and run as the large door swung open.

'Come in . . .' Julie said, holding the door open

then standing aside for her to enter. For a moment Diana felt like a fly invited into the spider's web. She had to remind herself that this was her idea.

She ventured inside. The door swung closed with a bang. The house was gloomy and badly lit. It smelt distinctly musty. A long staircase, carpeted in an almost threadbare Wilton, dominated the hallway.

'Let's go up,' Julie said. Her tone left no room for discussion. What was the point anyway? They both knew why Diana had come. 'Follow me.'

Meekly Diana mounted the stairs after her. Julie was small with short dark hair parted to one side like a man. She was not fat but her body was rectangular, strong and stout. She wore a plain black dress that reached to her knees. Diana watched her calves as they climbed the stairs. They looked muscled and strong like an athlete's.

The worn stair carpet only covered the middle of the treads. Either side the wood was painted brown. Like the paint on the front door this too was flaking. At the top of the stairs Julie led the way down a long hall. There were several doors, all of panelled wood. Diana noticed there was a key in the lock of every door. The light in the hall was weak, a single overhead brass chandelier with three bulbs set in green shades. Only one of the bulbs was working.

Julie stopped in front of one of the doors, her hand on the door knob.

'You didn't want polite small talk and a glass of wine did you?' she said, looking at Diana with eyes that appeared to be a cold colourless grey. 'I hate all that shit.'

'I don't want small talk,' Diana said, trying to sound as though she meant it. She was not at all sure what she wanted at that moment.

'Good. I do remember you, Diana. Very well. You're very beautiful. I wanted you then. But you weren't ready. You were just at the beginning. Now you're ready. I can feel it.'

She opened the door. If the corridor was dimly lit, this room was Stygian. It took a moment for Diana's eyes to adjust. There was a large four-poster bed, bedside table, a wardrobe and a chest that looked as though it might have been used by sixteenth-century pirates to bury treasure. The bed was covered with a black sheet. The walls were painted black too.

Julie closed the door. The only light in the room came from a old fashioned standard lamp draped with a black scarf.

'So . . .' Julie said, 'here we are.' She smiled. Her smile was crooked. It seemed to distort her face.

She picked up a packet of matches and lit what appeared to be a joss-stick. She set it into a small brass holder on the bedside table. The aroma from it was strong but it did not smell like incense.

'Come here, Diana.' Julie waved her over to the bed. 'Smell this . . . breathe it deeply. I'm so used to it . . . Smells heavenly . . .'

It did. Diana sat on the bed. It smelt wonderful. She lent forward to sniff again. She felt instantly light-headed as though someone had given her a large drink.

'Take your clothes off,' Julie said.

Diana breathed in again. The strange smoke, with a blue tint, filled her lungs. She felt a sudden sense of well-being, a great surge of warmth. The room was warm. She unbuttoned her red dress with no self-consciousness.

'Such beautiful breasts,' Julie said, as Diana unhooked her bra.

'I bought these at the shop,' Diana said indicating her underwear, hoping Julie would understand 'the shop' to mean where they had met, but not quite able to put that into words.

She couldn't remember taking her knickers off or her shoes and stockings but she must have because the next thing she knew she was lying in the centre of the black sheet looking down at her own naked body. It felt as though it belonged to someone else.

'Give me your hand,' Julie said.

Attached to each post of the bed was a thick tassled silk rope like the sort of cords used to tie back curtains. Julie wound one around Diana's outstretched wrist. The rope was black. It made Diana's arm seem very white by contrast.

'What are you doing?' Diana asked, feeling no alarm only delicious warmth and relaxation.

'I have to keep you secure...' Julie said. To Diana the explanation seemed perfectly plausible. Of course, she had to be secure.

Julie moved round the bed and tied Diana's other wrist. The rope felt soft and silky and not at all tight but Diana's arms were stretched out above her head.

'Open your legs now, Diana. Wide...' Julie ordered.

Suddenly Diana had the urge to giggle. 'You'll see my pussy,' she laughed. She couldn't remember ever using the word 'pussy' before.

'That's right.'

'Do you want to see my pussy, then?'

'Very much, Diana. It's very beautiful.'

'Yes it is.'

Diana splayed her legs apart. Julie wrapped the corded rope around her ankles one at a time. She stretched her legs tight apart.

'Does that feel nice, Diana?' she asked coming up to the top of the bed so she could stroke Diana's cheek with the back of her hand. 'Do you feel secure now?'

'Yes. Oh, yes . . . I feel delicious.'

Diana breathed in deeply, the intoxicating smoke making her feel more than just drunk. It was making her feel incredibly sexy. She moved her hand to stroke her sex but felt it held back. She tried her other hand but that was useless too. She tried to close her legs, rub her clitoris by moving her thighs but they wouldn't budge either. She couldn't understand why her arms and legs refused to respond but it didn't matter. Nothing mattered. She wriggled her bum on the bed and felt a little relief.

She couldn't see Julie.

'Julie?' she said.

'I'm here, darling, don't worry. I'm right here.' She came back into Diana's line of sight. She was carrying a little glass pot and a small brush like a make-up brush. 'Do you feel sexy?'

'Oh, very. Very. Oh, Julie. I feel so sexy . . .' she said and meant it. Her whole body seemed to be awash with a pure sexual pleasure.

'Good.'

131

Julie knelt on the bed, dipped the brush into the pot, wiped off the excess on the lip of the glass and applied the brush to Diana's nipple. Curiously, despite her feelings, neither nipple was erect. The brush provoked them. Julie covered both with the gelantinous liquid. It looked like honey but was thicker.

'Mmm...' Diana moaned as she felt her nipples wetted.

Julie moved down between her legs. She dipped the brush again and coated the whole of Diana's sex in the golden liquid. She took her time brushing into every crack and cranny.

Diana moaned again.

'Does that feel good?'

'Wonderful.' She wanted to ask what it was but didn't have the energy. Besides she wasn't at all sure the voice she heard answering Julie's questions was her voice. It sounded different, deeper, richer.

Julie moved out of sight again. Diana was sure if she lifted her head she would be able to see her but she didn't have the energy for that either.

Then the light went out which made the attempt academic. She thought she heard the door open and close again but she couldn't be sure. And didn't care.

Her nipples reacted first. To start with it was almost a stinging sensation, like the sting of a nettle, hot but not as sharp, not as painful. There was pain but a pain suffused with pleasure. Then the stinging went away and a heat, a deep penetrating heat, started. By the time the heat began in her nipples the crease of her sex was stinging,

harder than her nipples had, more acutely. It was
unpleasant and pleasant at the same time. She
would have loved to be able to scratch the itch. At
the same time it was exciting that she couldn't,
that she was prevented from touching herself. The
pleasantness took over. Now it was entirely
pleasant.

Suddenly it was as though there was only three
parts to her body, her two nipples and her cunt.
She strained against her bonds, not because she
wanted to touch herself but because she wanted to
feel her constriction. The silky ropes held her tight.
The iron claws in velvet gloves.

The heat penetrated deeper and deeper. It was
getting hotter. She closed her eyes but the room
was so dark there was no difference whether her
eyes were open or closed. Her cunt was throbbing.
Her mind was still befuddled. She couldn't piece
together what had happened to her, how she had
got here, naked, spread-eagled on this black sheet
in this strange room. But she didn't feel any alarm.
All she could feel was pleasure, pleasure from her
nipples and cunt, hot throbbing pleasure.

She was coming. She rolled her head from side to
side and struggled against the corded ropes bound
thickly around her wrists and ankles, not because
she wanted to escape but because the feeling of
helplessness was exciting her. She was open,
exposed, vulnerable. The heat was changing. Now
her nipples and every millimetre of her cunt felt
like a thousand butterflies were brushing their
wings against her most sensitive flesh.

Though there was no one to hear, she moaned,
'Yes, oh yes.'

It was not like any orgasm she had had before. It felt as if her cunt was alive, like it was dancing, her flesh throbbing, her clitoris going wild, and her nipples joining in. It felt like they had been tenderised, sensitised, so every sensation she felt was amplified into huge waves of pleasure. Her orgasm exploded through her body and she bucked herself against her bonds. She desperately wanted to touch herself but, at the same time, she knew her inability to do so, the feeling of being bound and spread open, was adding to the depth of the waves that pounded through her.

She was sweating. Sweat ran down her breasts. Sweat ran into her navel, pooling in her belly button. Another orgasm was taking over or perhaps it was the same one. Her body was stretched taut. The feelings created by whatever Julie had painted on her were changing again. No longer the little subtle brushing. The heat was returning. The heat of sex. Her flesh got hotter, a singular type of heat, heat concentrated only on her sexual organs, a wonderful pulsing heat. Her body shook as her orgasm took her over, this one harder, pulsing deeper. And immediately it allowed her down, allowed her conscious thoughts again, as opposed to sheer all-excluding pleasure, she felt a third orgasm beginning its circle in her body, a very short circle. She was spread-eagled on a rack of pleasure, tormented by pleasure, as the circle joined and another explosion racked through every nerve, nerves already singing with what had gone before.

She screamed. She heard her voice screaming. It seemed to echo, screaming back at her.

It was like a fever, the crisis of a fever. Then the crisis passed. Diana opened her eyes. The feeling of drunkenness had gone entirely. She felt sober. She raised her head and looked down at her body and only then realised the light was on again and the joss-stick on the bedside table had been snuffed out. Julie was standing naked by the side of the bed. Diana had no idea how long she had been there.

Her hand reached out and touched Diana's nipple. Her hand was cold, her touch so welcome Diana almost swooned with pleasure. Julie was holding a little bowl of warm water and a sponge. Gently, so gently Diana thought she might come again because of it, Julie sponged clean each nipple, removing the residue of whatever she had brushed on to them. Then she sponged the long crease of Diana's sex, delving into every crevice, taking her time, feeling Diana's body react, tiny tremors of pleasure making Diana gasp and quiver.

'Oh, that feels so good,' Diana said.

With a small towel, Julie dried Diana's body.

'Was it good?' she asked.

'Yes.'

Julie's hand rested on Diana's sex. Her middle finger crooked into her clitoris rubbing it from side to side very gently.

'Do you want me to untie you?'

'No . . .' Diana said. It was the last thing she wanted.

'Do you want me to stop?'

'No . . . please don't.' Even after the multiple orgasms Diana could still feel her body's need. They had been a prelude. She had been drugged, drunk.

Now she wanted to experience the real thing quite sober.

'What do you want, Diana?' Julie's voice betrayed no emotion.

'I want you to take me. I want to feel you. God, I'm so randy. You've made me feel so bloody sexy.'

Julie's finger increased its pressure on Diana's clitoris. She bent forward and, with the tip of her tongue, flicked at Diana's nipple. Diana moaned. Julie got up on to the bed and knelt between Diana's out-stretched legs. Diana remembered seeing the small breasts in the changing room of the lingerie shop. They were round and neat, their nipples small too but hard now, and a pinky red.

'Is this what you want?' Julie held up a U-shaped flesh-coloured rubber object. She saw Diana's expression of puzzlement. Immediately, she applied one end of the horse-shoe to her sex then pushed it home. She pushed it deep into herself until the other end projected from her body like a cock. It was shaped like a cock, a rough sculpture of a glans at its peak. The middle where the two ends met, now resting against Julie's pubis, was bulbous and shaped like two balls. The rubber had even been distressed to resemble pubic hair. Julie had grown a cock, a big thick cock.

'Is this what you want?' she repeated.

'Yes.'

Diana could see a flush of excitement coursing through Julie's body. Julie's pubic hair was almost as thick as Diana's. In the dim light of the room, with her short cut hair and almost shapeless breasts, Julie looked like a man.

Julie moved forward until the tip of the double

dildo was between Diana's labia. To her surprise
the dildo felt warm. She tried to worm her way
down on to it but the silk ropes held her tight.

Julie reached forward with her hands and gathered up the big mounds of flesh of Diana's breasts,
kneading them between her fingers.

'Fuck me,' Diana said. Whatever Julie had
painted on her was still having an effect. Her clitoris had never felt so sensitive. The head of the
dildo and Julie's fingers rubbing over her nipples
were making her faint with delight. Her sex felt
raw, as if layers had been stripped away to expose
the ultimate sensation.

Julie teased her. She pulled back, then nudged
forward and down, parting Diana's labia, but not
penetrating further. She held her buttocks together
tightly to hold the other end of the dildo firmly in
place. Julie had used the instrument before. It was
the best. To fuck and be fucked at the same time.
She filled it with a creamy warm liquid. If she
squeezed the bulb between the two ends the dildo
would even spunk. Like a man. She wished she
had a cock like a man but at the same time was
glad she hadn't. She would never get these feelings
as a man.

With a thrust of her hips Julie pushed the dildo
forward into the wringing wetness of Diana's cunt.
She stroked it in and out slowly, feeling the effect
in her own sex as pressure and counter-pressure
created the sensations she loved so much. As she
ploughed it forward, her end was levered back,
pushing into the soft walls of her sex. As she pulled
it out it felt like it was moving up inside her. She
pushed forward hard until she could feel Diana's

clitoris against her own. She wriggled her body
sideways so their clitorises rubbed on each other.

She had waited so long for this beautiful woman
to come to her. She had waited and imagined her.
She had never doubted Diana would come. One
day.

Julie's thrusts were faster now as her passion
mounted and Diana writhed under her, arching her
hips off the bed to meet her as she would with a
man. Julie's hands were still digging into her
breasts, her palms against her tender nipples. She
was using the breasts like handles, to pull herself
into Diana's body, her back curved like a bow to
ram the dildo home.

Diana and Julie were coming together. As the
source of their pleasure was the same, the same
instrument down between their legs, the same sensation, it was not surprising that their excitement
climbed the peaks together. In Diana's mind she
saw herself tied and spread. She saw a look in
Julie's eye, a look of sheer unadulterated lust. Each
thrust drove her higher, and drove Julie too. One
on one. She could feel Julie's body racked and trembling, nerve to nerve, with her own. She heard her
voice, gasping, shouting, panting, 'Do it, do it . . .'
over and over again just as Julie was saying 'Yes,
yes, yes.'

Before she lost control completely Julie's hand
found the bulb of the dildo and squeezed hard. Both
women simultaneously felt the hot creamy liquid
spurt into the depths of their cunt, the secret dark
caverns where men had spunked and spasmed for
them. The wetness took them over the edge,
pushed them from the peak they had reached so

that they were tumbling down the cliff, a tangled mess of legs and breasts and cunts, of labia and clitoris, joined by the warm wet dildo.

When Diana opened her eyes again she was free. Julie was lying besides her on the bed her head resting on her shoulder. She had an urgent desire to pee.

'I need the loo,' she said.

'Second door on the left,' Julie said rolling off Diana's body.

Diana got off the bed. She was a little unsteady on her feet but she managed to find her way out into the corridor. In a strange house her nakedness suddenly made her feel self-conscious. She quickly went up to the second door on the left and grasped the handle. The door did not budge. It was locked. There was no key on the outside as she'd noticed in some of the other doors. Perhaps someone was in there. She listened but could hear nothing.

Maybe Julie had meant the second door from the top of the stairs. Diana tried that door. There was a key in its lock but the door opened as she turned the handle. She looked inside. Unlike the room she had just left, this room was brightly lit and painted entirely in white. Even the floor was white linoleum. The only furniture was a single bed and a bedside table. Lying on the bed was a woman, at least Diana assumed it was a woman though there was no positive way to tell. The body was swathed in crepe bandages, from head to foot, wound round and round, over legs and thighs and chest. If it was a woman she either had small breasts or the bandages held them so tight against her ribs that they made no significant bulge. The only flesh visible was a tiny section of nose, the nostrils sticking out from the bandages that wreathed the head.

Diana stared, frozen by the spectacle. On the white bedside table was the little glass pot and brush, either the same one Julie had used on her or identical.

From the middle of the bandages a small black wire trailed off the bed, across the floor and into a transformer plugged into a wall socket. About a foot from the bed there was a switch in the black wire. Diana knew she should close the door and flee. But curiosity got the better of her. She tiptoed across the room and reached down to the switch. She hesitated. Then her fingers flicked the white button on the switch. The room was filled with a muffled buzzing, like the noise of a vibrator. The body on the bed, and Diana was certain it was a woman now she was close to it, rocked slightly from side to side. It was the only movement the bandages would allow. Diana heard a moan stifled by the crepe.

She was seized with a feeling of panic. She switched off whatever machine was attached to this human package, ran out of the room closing the door firmly behind her and hurried back into the bedroom, her desire to pee completely vanished. She looked around in the darkness for her clothes, her eyes having to readjust to the dimness again.

'I have to go,' she said finding her knickers on the floor and disentangling them from her suspender belt and stockings. She shimmied them up her legs and hooked on her bra.

'I hoped you'd stay longer,' Julie said. She sat up on the bed. 'There's a lot more I wanted to show you.' She had not taken the dildo out of her body so she still looked like a man with a powerful erection. Her hand encircled it and she was moving it up and down very slightly, like a man wanking.

'Sorry, I have to go.'

'This is just the beginning . . .'

Diana didn't bother with stockings. It would take too long to put them on. She just wanted to get out of the house.

'Would you mind if I didn't show you out? I feel so . . .' she looked down at the dildo in her hand, 'relaxed.'

'I remember the way. Don't worry.' Diana winkled her feet into her shoes and stuffed the stockings and suspender belt into her handbag. She went to the door.

'Don't I get a kiss?' Julie said pouting.

Diana walked back to the bed and pecked her on the cheek with as much enthusiasm as if she were kissing a snake. As she turned to go, Julie caught her wrist. Her grip was strong. She pulled Diana's hand on to her breast, then up to her mouth where she pressed the palm into her lips and Diana felt her tongue, hot and wet, lick it.

'Bye,' she said releasing the wrist.

'Bye,' Diana replied and rushed out.

She got to the front door with enormous relief and slammed it decisively after her.

Sitting in her car she felt better. Her heart was pounding but it slowly returned to normal. She had no idea why she had panicked, why the woman lying in the bandages had given her such a rush of what could only be described as fear. She didn't know and she didn't care. She was only glad she had escaped from the house and from Julie.

The sex had been sensational, her body still tingled with the feeling of it. It still bore the marks. Her wrists and ankles were ingrained with the pattern of the corded ropes. Her nipples and clitoris still felt incredibly sensitive, every movement reminding her of their tender condition. It had been an experience she would never forget.

But the more she thought about what Julie had done to her, the more she saw herself tied down on that black sheet, completely helpless, the more grateful she was that she had run out when she had. While she still could. What else Julie wanted to show her she could not imagine. What did the other rooms in the corridor contain?

Julie had released her. But what if she hadn't? There was no way she could have escaped from that bed on her own. A cold shiver ran through her body, extinguishing the last of her sexual heat.

She drove home quickly wanting to put as much distance between herself and Julie. She was delighted to think that Julie didn't have her address or telephone number.

It had been one adventure too many. One step too far. Diana knew she never wanted to see Julie again.

Chapter Six

It was a beautiful early autumn day. The sun shone through the windows of her bedroom and Diana lay in bed drinking the coffee Charles had brought her.

In the sunlight it was difficult to understand how the strange apprehensions of last night had taken such a hold on her. She fingered her nipples and clitoris under the bedclothes and found them still unusually sensitive. But apart from that, and finding herself thinking about the woman in bandages, her experience with Julie had left no lasting effects.

At eleven she drove to her exercise class and an hour of strenuous aerobics and sweat, together with the brisk fresh air, made her feel entirely restored.

Certainly Julie had made her forget all about her problems with the bank and her mortgage. During her work-out she had decided that there was only one way to solve that particular problem. It was, after all, the only option open to her: she was going to have to tell the truth. Well, something like the truth anyway.

After a hot shower Diana lunched in the health

club on fruit salad and mineral water and drove
home to change for her appointment with the
bank.

At three forty-five she parked her car in the
small car-park off the High Street and walked into
the bank.

'I have an appointment with Mr Appleby at four,'
she told the young boy who had come to the
ENQUIRIES window.

'I'll tell him you're here, Mrs . . .'

'Wilson.'

'If you'd come through into the waiting room . . .'

A buzzer sounded and the door beside the counter opened. The young boy beckoned Diana
through. She could see his eyes looking at her
appreciatively, though under the thick fur coat
there was little to see. Her high heels – they were
very high, their heels spiked and tipped with silver
– clacked on the wood-tiled floor as she walked
along the corridor, following the boy.

The waiting room smelt of stale cigarette smoke.
There were one or two posters on the walls adver-
tising the bank's services.

Diana did not sit down. She picked up a maga-
zine and flicked through it without really seeing
the pages.

'Ms Wilson . . .' the manager said as he opened
the waiting room door no more than five minutes
later. 'Sorry to keep you waiting.'

'I think I was early . . .'

'This way . . .' He led her into his office and indicated the chair in front of his desk. 'Would you like
coffee or tea?' He asked, before he sat down behind
his reproduction partner's desk.

'Coffee would be nice,' she said.

'Black? White?'

'Black, no sugar.'

Appleby picked up the phone and pressed one of the buttons. 'Deirdre, could you get me a tea and a coffee please, black no sugar.' He put the phone down. 'Would you like to take your coat off. It must be hot. These buildings are always over-heated. There seems to be no way to get it turned down.'

'In a minute, perhaps.'

'So, what have you got for me?' He looked genuinely enthusiastic at the prospect of learning what she had to say.

'I thought the best way to give you an idea of my new venture would be a sort of demonstration.'

'Yes, that's an excellent idea.' He opened the buff file on his desk. 'So we're dealing with a service industry . . .' he said, reading his notes.

'We work on a one-to-one basis.' Diana had crossed her legs in the chair. Her fur had fallen away to reveal the sheer shiny black nylon she was wearing. How far he could see up her legs she had no way of knowing, but she saw him looking.

'I wrote the word "fantasy" in my notes I see. I'm not entirely sure what that means.'

'That's why I thought a demonstration . . . We all have fantasies don't we?'

'What sort of fantasies?'

'Winning the pools. Going to romantic places. Taking out beautiful women . . .'

A heavy knock rattled the frosted glass of the office door.

'Come in, Deirdre . . .' the manager said.

A tiny frail-looking girl came in carrying a small

battered wooden tray on which were two cups and saucers, one filled with black viscous liquid that looked as though a layer of grease floated on the surface. She set the tray down on the manager's desk.

'Thank you,' he said.

'Right, sir,' she said closing the door behind her.

'I'm not really sure what you're getting at,' Appleby said picking the coffee cup off the tray and setting it down on the corner of the desk nearest to Diana.

Diana picked up the cup and sipped the black liquid. It tasted as though dirty washing-up water had been mixed with tar. She tried not to let her disgust show.

'Well. Take us, now. I mean you're a very attractive man. You're fit, healthy. I might fantasise about you. And vice versa. I'm sure you find me attractive, don't you?'

'You're an exceptionally attractive woman, of course but . . .'

'Thank you. And?'

'I don't see . . .'

'Don't you have fantasies about me?'

'Ms Wilson, that would be most . . .'

'I know, I know. I'm not talking about sexual harassment. But be truthful. Really truthful. Can you really tell me you haven't thought about what it would be like, for instance, to take me out to dinner . . .?'

Appleby smiled. 'Of course, I think it's perfectly natural that I should . . .'

'To sit looking into my eyes all evening. To kiss me . . .'

'I'm sure every man you meet...'

'To fuck me. Tell me truthfully, Mr Appleby. Haven't you ever imagined what it would be like to fuck me?'

That was the point of no return, Diana knew. Appleby would either clear his throat, sit forward in his chair, pick up her file and tell her that they should get back to business, that that was quite enough of that, and had she brought in the cash flow projections and all the other accounts of her new business as previously discussed? Or. Or...

There was a long silence before he said anything, her last words 'fuck me' seemed to hang in the air.

He leant back in his swivel chair and laced his hands behind his head.

'The truth?'

'Yes.'

'The truth is, I think you are one of the most exciting women I've ever met. Of course I've thought of what it would be like to...' he couldn't quite bring himself to say 'fuck' so he settled for, 'go to bed with you. But I don't see the relevance to what we are supposed to be discussing...'

'But that's not all is it?'

'What do you mean?'

'If you've really thought about me since yesterday, haven't you thought about what you'd like to do with me?'

'Other than going to bed you mean?' He was hooked now, she could see it in his eyes, thinking about everything she said, imagining it.

'Yes, what we would do in bed...'

Diana got up and went to the office door. A small

147

brass bolt was positioned above the door handle. She shot it, then turned back to Appleby.

'Have you imagined what I look like, my body? Have you imagined what I am wearing under this coat?'

'I . . .'

She slipped the coat off her shoulders and it slid to the floor. The black basque, constructed in lace and satin, was, she knew, the most flattering lingerie for her. It emphasised her large breasts, pushing them up and together into a tunnel of cleavage. It emphasised her pinched waist which it cinched in tightly. It left the flare of her hips and the rich curves of her buttocks bare. Its long suspenders, reaching over her navel and down her flanks to pull at the black welts of her stockings, made her long legs seem even longer. Above the tops of the stockings her thighs seemed creamy and exposed in contrast to the black that framed them.

She turned to let him see her arse. The basque ended abruptly in the small of her back. Her tight, pert buttocks were naked, bisected only by a thong of nylon, buried deep in the cleft of her arse, from the tiny panties she wore, no more than a triangle of lace strung on narrow straps of nylon.

She faced him again. The panties hardly contained the thick hair of her pubis. He could see it down between her legs covering her labia.

'Haven't you ever fantasised about a woman coming into your office, locking the door, slipping off her fur, looking like this. Then coming round your desk . . .' Diana moved around the desk and caught Appleby's thick curly black hair in her hand, wrenching his head back quite hard so he was star-

ing up into her face. 'Someone who wanted you.
Needed you. Forced you.' She pushed his head into
her cleavage then pulled it back again by his hair
and kissed him hard on the mouth, plunging her
tongue between his lips.

The swivel chair he was sitting on had rolled
back against the window ledge behind his desk.
Diana sat across his lap then yanked his head back
from her mouth.

'I like to take what I want. Haven't you ever
imagined that?'

'Yes . . .' he said breathlessly. Pulling his hair had
brought tears to his eyes. She could feel his erection
struggling to escape the constriction of his trousers.

'I want you to fuck me.' She dropped to her knees
in front of him and pulled the zip of his flies down.
She groped inside to release his cock. It sprung
from his trousers like a jack-in-the-box. She pulled
his foreskin back and plunged her mouth down on
it, sucking his cock hard, wanting to make him
moan, her long hair sweeping his lap. Then she
pulled her mouth away and started nibbling at the
side of his cock, biting it with her teeth.

'This is a fantasy, isn't it? A woman doing this
to you,' she said, between bites, 'in your office, in
the middle of the day.'

'Yes,' he gasped.

'Now, fuck me.' She stood up and turning round,
bent over his desk, pushing his papers aside with
her elbows, and opening her legs. He would be able
to see the whole of her sex, her swollen labia,
fringed with pubic hair, the bud of her anus, the
long curve of her buttocks. She reached behind her
to pull the thong of the black panties aside then

looked over her shoulder to watch him stand up, unbuckle his belt and pull his trousers and pants down to his knees, the tails of his shirt on either side of his erection.

'My fantasy . . .' he said in a voice that sounded quite different from the measured tone he had used before. 'You want to know my fantasy . . .'

He raised his arm high in the air and brought his palm swinging down onto the cheek of her arse. The resounding smack of flesh on flesh echoed through the office. 'My fantasy . . .' he repeated, swinging his arm again and landing a second blow on the flesh already reddened from the first.

Almost before Diana could react to the two stinging slaps Appleby had pushed himself on to her, his cock hard and hot between her legs. The nylon thong of the panties had slipped back into place. He grabbed it to pull it out of his way but used so much force it snapped and came away in his hand. He bucked his hips back, then thrust forward, his cock sliding into her wet cunt so smoothly it was as though they had practised the movement a hundred times.

Diana wriggled her bum against his shirt tails feeling the length of his cock inside her. The pain from the blows of his hands had turned immediately to pleasure, a tingling warm pleasure spreading over her arse. What had started as a performance, what she had rehearsed in her mind this morning was no longer a question of acting. Appleby was thrusting into her with an urgency she couldn't ignore. She couldn't play her part any more. She could only react to what he was doing to her.

His hands were all over her thighs, feeling the tops of her stockings, fingering her suspenders as if he couldn't believe they were real. Then one hand moved up to her breasts, squeezing them under the lacy cups of the basque, then pushing the material aside so her breast hung free and he could get at the nipple with his finger and thumb.

Diana supported herself on her elbows her head looking down at the desk. If she had cared to, she could read her own bank statement in the file underneath her.

Appleby moved his hands over her long slender back divided by the tight black basque. He started gathering up her long hair, combing it into a pony tail with his fingers, catching every last strand until he held it all in one hand.

Then as he stroked his cock in and out of her silky cunt he pulled her hair back, forcing her to lift her head, like a horse on a rein, her back arched, the long curve of her spine like an archer's bow.

He was not gentle with her. He jerked her hair back. With his other hand he slapped her flank hard, like slapping a horse. She was his horse and he was riding her.

The second time he slapped her she knew she could not stop herself from coming. He was so powerful, so hard, his cock so urgent. He'd taken control, held her, shaped her, done what he wanted to do. She felt her head pulled back, her neck taut, her buttocks hot and stinging and his cock so deep in her she could feel it at the neck of her womb. Her body could stand no more. Her nerves exploded, sensation rolled over her and she stood, pressing herself into the desk for support, her whole body quivering and trembling as her orgasm took control of her every reflex.

He felt what he had done to her. It would have been difficult not to. He could still feel it. Her cunt was contracting around him, like the gills of a fish out of water. He had wanted to prove something to her. That he wasn't a dull little man working in a dull little bank who could be teased and used. He wanted to prove he was a man. Now he would use her, use her beauty, all her deliberate provocation, use it to drive himself higher, to get his spunk deeper, to have his completion.

He found his place in the wet walls of her tight clinging cunt. He stopped pummelling into her. He waited, quite still, knowing that his body would do the rest. He felt his cock starting to spasm, felt his orgasm exploding in him, his eyes rolling back in his head, his spunk spraying out into the space he had found, hot and uncontrolled. It seemed to go on forever.

Neither of them moved. His cock begun to shrink. He loosened his grip on her hair, stroking it softly as it slipped through his fingers.

'Well, Mr Appleby,' Diana said, finally straightening up when she felt his cock slide from the wetness of her sex. 'It seems you have a very active imagination.'

He pulled up his trousers and slumped back into his chair. He seemed not to care that his shirt was not properly tucked in. Diana caressed his cheek with the back of her hand then walked around the desk, picked up the fur off the floor and put it back on. The torn black panties had fallen neatly into the open file on his desk.

'Now do you understand my cash flow?'

'Yes.'

'And do I get my mortgage?'

'Well . . .'

'Well, what?'

'If it were up to me . . .'

'Isn't it?'

'Oh yes. Yes. But it has to be passed by the area manager. I'll recommend it. Naturally. You can rely on that. But he has to pass it . . .'

'Yes . . .'

'And without figures, accounts, projections. I mean after what you've just shown me I'm quite sure the bank's money is absolutely safe. There's no question about that. But head office are more . . . stringent.'

'Why don't you get me an appointment with the area manager then?'

'No, no. He never sees the general public. There's no need. That's not his job. He just looks at the recommendations we put forward, checks all the figures . . . that sort of thing. Obviously, in your case there are no figures to check. My recommendation will carry some weight. I can say you're a highly valued customer, always in credit, etc . . . but it may not be enough. I can hardly tell him why I'm so convinced can I?'

'But if I could . . .'

'He wouldn't see you.'

'Couldn't you try?'

'He won't. That's all there is to it.'

'So what do you suggest?' Diana said. Everything had gone so well up to this point. She'd imagined the mortgage was just a formality. It seemed she couldn't have been more wrong. 'There must be some way.'

He thought for a moment his mind still full of images of their bodies locked together over his desk.

'Could I go to his home?' She prompted.

'God, no. He's married. Three children. Wife. Nanny.' He lapsed into thought again. 'There is one thing . . .'

'What?'

'He's coming up to London next week. The area office is Winchester you see. De-centralisation. The bank moved head office out to the sticks a few years ago. But he has to come up to town next week.'

'And he stays in a hotel?'

'Always the same one. The bank has a special arrangement with them. The Royal Palm in Kensington. You know it?'

'Yes.'

'If you were to . . .'

'Will he be alone?'

'Definitely. If you . . .'

'I can work out the rest for myself. Next week. All next week?'

'Monday to Friday.'

'And his name?'

'Carlton. Michael Carlton.'

'Thank you. I'm sure I can do something to persuade him.'

'Good luck. He's got a reputation in the bank as being a mean so-and-so. He even counts the paperclips.'

'Am I allowed one more question?'

'What's that?'

'What's your name?'

'Barry.'

'Well, Barry. Thank you again. For everything. I had no idea bank managers could be so... inventive.'

'I had no idea customers could be so provoking.'

There was a heavy knock at the office door.

'Come...' Appleby was about to say before Diana raised her finger to her lips to stop him. She got up quickly, unbolted the little brass bolt, then slipped back into her seat.

'Come in,' Appleby called.

Deirdre opened the door.

'Finished with the cups, sir?' she said.

'Yes, thank you.'

The liquid in both cups remained undrunk. A lot of it had splashed into the saucers and over the tray and desk as their bodies had knocked into the furniture.

'What a mess,' Deirdre commented. She looked around for something to mop up the spillage until her eyes lighted on the black panties lying in the middle of the buff file right in front of her manager's face.

Appleby reacted instantly, smartly closing Ms Wilson's file on Ms Wilson's panties.

Chapter Seven

Ann and Diana had taken care over what they wore. Ann had chosen a dark blue velvet dress. Though it was strapless its skirt was full length, with a deep kick pleat to make walking easier, since the material was cut to hug her legs. Diana wore a dress made of material that looked as though it had been spun with gold. It fitted her rich bosom tightly and followed the line of her waspy waist but then flared out into a full pleated skirt. The neckline of the dress was unusual. From one side of the throat it was cut diagonally down to the top of her bust. One arm and one shoulder was completely bare, while the other arm and shoulder were completely covered in the shimmering gold.

They had opened a bottle of champagne and, with Charles consigned to his bedroom, sat drinking and talking. At exactly eight o'clock Diana heard the crunch of tyres of the gravel drive. Looking through the curtain she saw a silver-grey Rolls-Royce park behind her car in the drive.

'Rolls,' she said to Ann.

'Must be loaded.'

'John said he was.'

'Rich, old and infirm, no doubt,' Ann said, looking glum.

'Not necessarily.'

'Want a bet?'

Diana opened the front door before John Borland could ring the doorbell. The man beside him was neither old nor infirm.

'This is Stewart Hood,' John said kissing her on the cheek. 'Stewart Hood, Diana Wilson.'

'Hi there, darling,' the man said in a Texas accent as thick as brown toast. He picked the ten-gallon white stetson he was wearing, off his head. 'Just call me Tex. I'm sure you can guess why.'

'Please to meet you, Tex. Come in, come in . . .'

Diana led them into the living room.

'And this is my friend, Ann Connell. Stewart Hood.' Diana looked straight into Ann's eyes and grinned an expression that said 'I told you so'.

'Tex,' he corrected, taking Ann's hand and kissing it. 'Well, my God, you're a fine-looking woman, if I ever saw one.'

'And, John, this is Ann.'

'I've heard so much about you,' he said.

'And I've heard everything about you,' Ann replied. They shook hands rather formally.

Diana handled round glasses of champagne. It was obvious that Stewart was just as struck with Ann as she was with him. For most men Ann's height presented a challenge but not for Tex. Tex's big frame gave him considerable height. He was a big man in every way though Diana had the impression that the thickness of his body and limbs came from muscle rather than fat. He seemed to

158

exude a sort of strength and power. His hair was
cut in a short crew cut, flecked with grey, it was
thick and wiry. He had bunches of hair growing
from his ears and the back of his hands were
covered with hair so thick it was almost like animal
fur. His face was lined and weather-worn with a
complexion so tanned it was obvious he spent a
great deal of his time in the sun. His eyes were
deep set and a dark brown.

'So you're in oil?' Ann asked.

'What makes you say that?'

'Texas . . . stetson . . .'

He laughed. 'But you forgot my boots . . .'

He pulled up the knees of his trousers to reveal
a pair of tan leather riding boots with squared toes.
Cowboy boots but not fancy silver-capped, snake-
skinned ones; these were used.

'I'm in cattle.'

'Oh . . .'

'A cowboy?' Diana said.

'He's not a cowboy. He owns a bloody great ranch
outside Santa Fé. About a million head of cows . . .'
John explained.

'That doesn't mean I'm not a cowboy. I still ride
the range, boy. Every day.'

'In London?' Ann teased.

'Sure thing. I ride in Hyde Park when I'm over
here. Every day.'

'How interesting,' Ann said, her eyes not having
left Tex for more than a moment since he came
into the room.

'And I go to the rodeo. I can rope a calf in thirty-
two seconds . . .'

'Do what?'

159

'Lasso a calf, roll it over and hogtie ...'

'Oh, I think I've seen that in the movies.' Ann said.

'Sure. Thirty-two seconds ...'

'You must be very strong.'

'Ah, there's a trick to it.'

'And is it hot in Texas?'

'Sure thing. Real hot. It's a lot different from London. This place hasn't got the space to throw a rope and there's so many people. In Texas we've got space and no people.'

Diana got up and refilled her guests' glasses.

'So where did you two meet?' she asked John.

'My company sent me over to Texas and we met in a bar in Dallas ...'

'The Hogtied Inn ...' Tex said laughing.

'Sounds very romantic,' Ann teased.

'Oh, it sure was. Forty sweaty cowboys who'd been on the trial for a week and hadn't bathed or changed their clothes the whole damn time. That place smelt higher than a skunk on heat.'

'What were you doing there?' Ann asked John.

'Oh, I'm in the brewery business. My company wanted to buy a brewery in the southern states. I went around looking for one. I seemed to spend a lot of time in bars. Tex has got a half share in the one we eventually bought.'

'So now he's goin' to have to learn all about our little Texas customs. Snake bites and Indians. First thing, he's got to buy some good boots ...'

'Can you ride?' Diana asked.

'I know the front end from the back,' John said.

'Well, I need to chucker down folks. My belly thinks my throat's been cut.'

'Where are we going?' Ann asked.

'The Conna...'

'No, actually,' John interrupted. 'We've organised a little surprise.' He winked at Diana. 'Don't worry, the food's sensational.'

Ann took Tex's strong muscled arm and they led the way out to the car, picking her coat up on the way.

'He's very attractive...' Diana whispered to John, as he helped her into her fur.

'What did you expect? Some old duffer?'

'Exactly.'

'They're a good match. He dwarfs most women...'

'Don't be rude...'

'I'm not... she's gorgeous, big and glorious. I could go for her myself.'

'You've got your hands full with me.'

In the Rolls the two women sat in the back with John while Tex rode up front with the uniformed chauffeur. The big car glided noiselessly through the traffic while Tex, half-turned in his seat, kept up a seemingly endless barrage of stories about experiences on the wide open range where buffaloes used to roam.

It took twenty minutes to reach the restaurant. At first Diana thought that the driver had made a mistake. The car had drawn up in front of a church, its ornate façade neatly squeezed between two tall Georgian terraced houses.

The driver came round to the rear door and Diana climbed out first.

'It's a church,' she said.

'You said you wanted to go somewhere smart,' John explained as he joined her on the pavement.

'A church?'

Ann had been helped out of the car by Tex.

'A church?' she echoed.

At that moment one of the pair of heavy polished wooden doors opened and a uniformed commissionaire appeared.

'Good evening, Mr Hood,' he said.

'Hi there, Charley boy. Ladies . . .' Tex indicated the door. Ann looked quizzically at Diana then lead the way through the large ecclesiastical style doors. Instead of stepping into the echoing vastness of a church they found themselves in a small vestibule, thickly carpeted, with walls lined in red silk and an old Victorian pulpit chopped down to size to form a desk for the reservations book of the restaurant.

'May we take your coats, ladies. Your room is ready, Mr Hood,' the maître d' behind the lectern said. A girl stepped forward to help them out of their coats and take them away to a little alcove set under a spiral wooden staircase to their left. The wood of the staircase, the newel post and balustrades were obviously original to the building. It had been stripped and limed.

The maître d' lead the way up the staircase. Set in gold frames on the walls were antique menus of banquets and dinners from Edwardian times, dinners in honour of the Prince of Wales, banquets of ten courses, with fine wines, clarets from the 1890s, ports from 1850s and Armagnacs a great deal older.

At the top of the staircase there was a circular gallery where sofas and armchairs had been arranged to form a bar area. The bar was more or less full. Down below, under the ornately carved railings of the gallery, was the main restaurant. Above the ceiling rose into a vaulted arch, supporting, on massive wooden beams, what had once been the belfry of the small Victorian church.

The mâitre d' guided them through the richly decorated bar, passed the cocktail drinking customers and through into a narrow corridor. At the end of the corridor was a door that had been padded in green leather. He opened the door and stood aside for them to enter.

'The Green Room, Mr Hood, as requested.'

The room looked for all the world like the dining room of a large Victorian house. There was a large fireplace, in which a real log fire burnt brightly. The walls were painted a deep green with all the upholstery colour co-ordinated to match. At one end of the room, furthest from the fire, a large table was laid with white linen, gleaming glasses and sparkling silver. Candles, in silver candelabra, had already been lit, and their soft flickering glow added to the atmosphere of plush comfort. There were candles on the mantelpiece too and in holders mounted on all the walls.

'It's beautiful,' Diana exclaimed.

'This is the best,' Tex said.

Two sofas were positioned in front of the fire. Between them a mahogany occasional table bore a Georgian wine cooler, crystal wine flutes, a silver bowl of nuts and another of delicate canapés. The wine cooler contained a bottle of Krug champagne which the mâitre d' opened skilfully.

John sat on one of the sofas and patted the seat next to him to indicate that Diana should join him. Tex and Ann sat side by side on the other. The mâitre d' handed round the champagne.

'Have a pleasant evening, ladies and gentlemen,' he said bowing slightly as he took his leave.

'What is this place?' Ann asked.

'It's a club. They do a lot of corporate dining so they have these private rooms . . .' John explained.

'Great, ain't it?' Tex said. 'I love all this olde worlde stuff.'

'It's like the days when men took their mistresses to private rooms in restaurants,' Ann said.

'They did what?'

'In Victorian and Edwardian times. They used to eat, then lock the door and fuck,' Ann explained.

'Now that sounds civilised. Why don't we have restaurants like that anymore?'

'Sometimes they didn't bother to lock the doors,' Diana said.

'Hard on the waiters,' John added.

'Very hard.' Tex formed a circle with his forefinger and thumb.

At that moment a waiter entered and the foursome dissolved into laughter to the bemusement of the man, who stood waiting uneasily to hand out the menus.

The dinner was superb. They ate lavishly on oysters and game and vanilla soufflés. The wines matched the food, but were a great deal more expensive. Tex took delight in telling them the Chateau Petrus they were drinking cost £500 a bottle and the Chateau Yquem, which he ordered to go with the sweet soufflés, cost even more.

He was not presented with a bill at the end of the meal however, so Diana could not sneak a look at how much the evening had cost overall. Her idle curiosity would have to remain unsatisfied.

Over the coffee and a three-tiered platter of petits fours they returned to the sofas and the fire, which the waiters had stoked periodically during the meal.

'So what happens now?' Diana asked.

'The night is young,' Ann said.

'It's going to be difficult to top that meal,' John added.

'Well, if you're all game, it's back to my place. I've got a little apartment I'd like you all to see. And I've got some very old Armagnac just waiting to be drunk. Goes with the view of London ...'

The Rolls, magically it seemed, but no doubt summoned by someone in the restaurant, glided up to the doors of the former church.

'You two get in the back. Ann's going to sit up front on my knee.'

'I'm too heavy.'

'Honey, you're no heavier than a bull calf. I had one of those on my lap plenty of times ...'

As soon as they were installed in the car and it drove off into the traffic, Tex and Ann started kissing, deep tonguing kisses, Tex's hand moving over Ann's long velvet dress from top to bottom.

'They seem to have hit it off,' Diana whispered.

'If he puts his tongue any further down her throat she'll drown,' John said.

'Why don't you demonstrate?' Diana asked, leaning forward to be kissed, the spectacle in front of her eyes making her feel left out.

In the following flurry of kissing and caressing neither couple noticed the car pulling into Grosvenor Square and coming to rest outside an impressive mansion block. Discreetly the chauffeur got out of the car and left its occupants to their sport, leaning against the bonnet waiting for some sign that he should open the doors.

'Hey, guys, we've arrived.' Tex shouted, finally disengaging himself from Ann. 'Well, look at you two.'

In the back Diana had slid down the large leather bench seat with John half on top of her. Her skirt had ridden up to show an expanse of thigh and the clip of her suspender on one leg.

'Fornicating in public is illegal in Texas.'

Diana pulled herself into an upright position as John rolled off her on to the thick woollen rugs. She realised she was really quite drunk. With as much dignity as she could she pulled her skirt down to her knees.

'We were just being friendly,' she said.

'Hey, don't mind me, I enjoyed the view.'

They piled out of the car as the chauffeur hurried to open at least one of the doors. Tex let them into the foyer of the mansion block. It was as impressive as the exterior, a vast space with a pink marble floor and a sweeping marble staircase beside the glided cage of a lift.

In the lift Ann and Tex fell into an embrace. The lift rose, whizzing and clanking, to the top floor and opened into a hallway that appeared to have only one door.

'I have the whole floor,' Tex explained, fumbling for his keys.

The view of London was spectacular. The flat was vast and ultra modern, matching the expensive modern art; Hockney, Miro and Pollack hung on the walls. Tex made no comment on the paintings and led them into the living room where a wall of windows presented the panoramic view to its best advantage and huge white silk sofas were sunk into a rectangular pit in the middle of the room. The pit was equipped with the controls for the sound system and the lights as well as a fridge and bar.

Tex walked down the steps into the pit, laid out four balloon glasses, a bottle of 1949 Armagnac, put an Oscar Petersen CD into the sound system, dimmed the lights and pulled Ann down on to the sofa next to him, resuming the physical relationship that had started in the car.

Diana sat down on the sofa opposite and John sat besides her. They sipped at the dark golden brandy.

'Do you want coffee?' John asked.

'No. I feel a bit drunk but it's pleasant.'

She put her glass down and kissed him. He put his glass down too and soon they were as intwined as they had been in the Rolls except with a great deal more comfort. The room was filled with the tinkling sounds of piano over-laid with moans and gasps of pleasure.

Finally Tex came up for air. He had unzipped Ann's long dress to caress her back. As she sat up it fell to her waist to reveal the black strapless bra she was wearing. She made no attempt to hitch the dress back into place. After the experiences Ann and Diana had shared together over the last weeks, false modesty did not seem appropriate.

'Well, what d'you guys think?' Tex said brightly,

drinking his brandy in one gulp.

'This is your idea of a small apartment?' Diana asked, sitting up.

'Heck, in Sante Fé this looks like a chicken shed in the bayou. Now let me show you somethin'. I've got every gadget money can buy.'

He leant forward and touched a small console set in the table that separated the two vast sofas. Immediately, a screen dropped down in front of one of the Pollack paintings and the music stopped. He pressed another button. The screen lit up and resolved into a picture of a man chained to a wall in what appeared to be a medieval dungeon. Two women wearing black leather basques and thigh-length boots, were taking it in turns to whip the man with long thin whips. His backside was already criss-crossed with red welts.

'That gets the circulation going,' Tex said laughing. 'I've got every sort of pornography you care to name in this little box of tricks.'

He pressed the buttons on the console again. The picture faded to be replaced by the image of a naked woman. She was on her knees on a double bed being fucked from the rear by one man while she, in turn, sucked on the cock of a man who lay in front of her. As they watched, the man who had been fucking her pulled out of her cunt, wanked himself once or twice, then sprayed spunk all over her back.

'Wouldn't you rather have the real thing,' Ann said loudly, over the soundtrack of moans and gasps coming from the screen.

'This is the real thing, honey,' Tex replied.

Ann stood up. With a grace and elegance that

was purely accidental, her dark blue velvet dress cascaded to the floor, like a statue being unveiled. 'No Tex, this is the real thing.'

Both men stared at her near-naked body. The lacy black strapless bra that clung precariously to her breasts was matched by a thin black suspender belt and her tanga panties were cut so high on the hip they formed a V-shape across her pelvis.

She stepped out of the dress and stood on the low table between the two men pirouetting so they could see her body from the front and the back, her high heels and the sheer black stockings emphasising her long, long legs.

Like a man who was sleep-walking, Tex pressed a button on the console and the screen went blank, then wound itself back into the wall. He turned the dimmed lights up slightly.

Ann reached behind her back and unhooked her bra, holding the cups to her breasts once it was free, in a good imitation of a stripper, then throwing it off. She threw it at Tex's face. With good reflexes, he caught it in his teeth.

'I think she's had a little bit too much to drink.' John whispered to Diana.

'Ann . . .' Diana was not sure what to say. More than a little drunk herself she was caught up in watching Ann's delicious body herself.

'She's OK. She's OK. Let her be . . .' Tex didn't want the show to stop. 'You're OK aren't you, baby?'

'I feel great. Is this better than a porno film?' Ann was massaging her breasts with both hands. She pinched and played with her nipples until they were fully erect.

'Sure thing,' Tex said enthusiastically.

Leaving her breasts, Ann snaked her hands along her sides, smoothing her flesh with her palms as though trying to iron invisible wrinkles.

'Put the music on again,' she said.

Tex pressed a button on the console and Oscar Petersen resumed exactly where he had been interrupted before. Ann swayed her hips to the slow tempo, her hands caressing her flesh in large circles, the movement of each hand synchronised with the other. Then her fingers hooked into the top of her knickers. She slowly pulled them down over her hips and her stockinged thighs. On the right side the black silk snagged on one of her suspenders. Deftly she freed it. The triangle of black peeled away from her pubis revealing her wispy sparse pubic hair and the beginning of the crease of her sex. For a moment she left the knickers there, at the point where the apex of the pubic triangle pointing down, met the apex of the triangle of her knickers pointing up.

'More,' she asked, looking at Tex and knowing what his answer would be.

'You bet,' he said. He was sitting on the edge of the sofa looking like a boy on Christmas morning who'd been given exactly what he'd asked for.

Ann closed her legs and pulled the knickers down until they fell of their own accord to her ankles. She stepped out of them and with a flick of the shoe sent them flying into Tex's face. This time they landed on his nose and slid down his face. He had time to put out his tongue to catch them and drew them into his mouth.

'Mmm . . .' he said, as though savouring a tasty treat.

Ann sunk to her knees, knocking aside one of the oriental boxes that decorated the table. With one hand she stroked the curve of her pubic bone, while the other circled and petted her large round buttocks. Diana watched, as enthralled as the two men. Ann's hand spread her labia open with her fingers, stretching them wide open until they could all see the pink and crimson interior, while her other hand, from the back pushed two fingers deep into her cunt.

'I'm so hot,' she said. 'Hot and wet.'

It was obvious she was right; as she pulled her fingers out they glistened with her juices.

She levelled her eyes at Diana and gave her a look of lust combined with amusement and challenge.

'Let's give them a show,' she said calmly. 'I'm not drunk, Diana, I just feel so sexy . . .'

Diana had no need to ask what she meant. She knew exactly what Ann had in mind. They had done it before for an audience of two. No doubt, if she had had less to drink, if she had been thinking more clearly she might have hesitated, been inhibited, found reasons not to follow the instincts of her body, not to listen to its pulsing needs. Or that was what she tried to tell herself. The truth was, as she knew full well, it was not the drink that had loosened her inhibitions but everything that had happened to her in the last months. Now she was free. She did what she wanted, not what some out-dated, irrelevant social convention told her to do. Her only criteria now was what she wanted, what made her feel good, alive, open and independent.

Ann held out her hand from where she knelt on

the table. Diana got up from the sofa. She looked down at John, not for his approval but to see his reaction. His expression was difficult to read. He looked as though he were in a trance. His eyes moved from Ann's near naked body to Diana. He was looking at her body as though trying to imagine what it would look like next to Ann's.

Diana took Ann's hand in both of hers. She brought it up to her mouth. First she kissed her long fingers, then the soft flesh on the back of her hand. Then, one by one, she sucked each finger into her mouth, deep into her mouth, sucking it hard her lips formed into a perfect circle.

'Well, now,' Tex said. 'This is certainly going to be something to see. You've got the sort of friends I like, John boy . . .' There was no doubt as to Tex's attitude. He literally licked his lips, his eyes sparkling with excitement.

Diana took Ann's other hand and repeated the sucking of her fingers. On this hand the fingers tasted of Ann's juices, a taste Diana knew well.

'Tastes of you,' she muttered, with a finger in her mouth.

'Good . . .' Ann said getting up off the table to stand in front of her friends. She kissed Diana on the lips, not a long kiss but short pecking kisses, at least until Diana caught her cheeks in her hands and forced her into a longer, deeper kiss.

John Borland moved round to sit on the sofa next to Tex so he could get a better view.

'So these two are lessies?' Tex asked, as he saw Diana's tongue dart into Ann's mouth.

'Not as far as I know,' John said, as astonished by what he was seeing as the American.

172

Ann had gathered the skirt of Diana's dress in her fingers, reeling it in until she had a bunch of material in her hand, just below Diana's waist. Like her friend, Diana was wearing stockings, a metallic black and gold weave, with a slippery sheen that matched the gold dress. Like her friend too, she was wearing a thin black suspender belt, the straps pulled taut down the long contours of her thighs.

Diana stepped out of Ann's embrace to pull the dress over her head.

'Wowee!' Tex whistled, as Diana's tits, barely contained in her strapless bra, came into view. 'I mean I could tell she had big bosomers but they're really something. What a lucky dog, Johnny boy.'

Diana said nothing. She let Ann's hands reach behind her back and unhook the bra. As it fell away Ann buried her face in Diana's cleavage, a feeling she loved, licking and sucking at the quivering flesh. She pressed the breasts in from the sides, trapping her face between them.

'She's really got tits.' Tex still could hardly believe what was happening in front of his eyes.

John Borland said nothing. He watched fascinated as the exquisite body he had fucked was expertly handled by a woman. It was not a spectacle he had ever expected to see, but in one sense he was not surprised. Diana had shown him a capability for depths of sensuality he had never experienced in a woman and a total lack of inhibition. He was not astonished her sensuality and freedom extended to women as well as men.

Ann extracted her face from the mounds of flesh. Her hands released Diana's breasts and slid down

173

to her friend's side, following the waspy curve of her waist until her fingers lighted on her panties. Licking, sucking and nibbling, her mouth descended too, down over her flat belly. As she peeled Diana's knickers away her tongue followed the trail, her lips brushing the familiar forest of her pubic hair, as it sprung from the constriction of the silk, then dipped lower, as the silk fell away, to tongue the crease of her sex.

Using her tongue like a finger, Ann parted the pubic hair and probed her labia to tease out her clitoris. It was already swollen. Ann worked it delicately, as she had learnt to do, the tiniest of movements with the tip of her tongue, little circles, little taps, little nudges. She knew by now what pleased her friend: she knew it because it was exactly what pleased her. She could feel Diana respond too, her hands holding Diana's hips firmly.

A tableau, a modernist chair shaped from female flesh.

Diana was coming. Her panties around her ankles, Ann's tongue barely touching her clitoris, the faintest of touches; it didn't matter. It was enough. More than enough. This was her fantasy. It had always been her fantasy. Being watched. It was buried in her sexual psyche. When she had been young, it was one of her first experiences; a man had burst into the bedroom where her boyfriend had been fucking her. She had seen him look at them, look at her, her legs splayed open. It had made her come. Harder and faster than ever before. She could still see the look in his eyes ten years later. It was the same now. Ann's tongue was expert but it was the look in the men's eyes that was

174

bringing her off. In John's eyes, who knew her, knew what she was capable of, and in the American's, who did not, who was a stranger.

'I'm coming,' she said, wanting them all to know. 'You're making me come.'

The words themselves took her over the edge. As much as she wanted to watch the men, her orgasm forced her eyes to close, forced her to remember the look in their eyes, as her body locked, her nerves screaming with absolute pleasure and she felt Ann's hands on her hips digging into her soft flesh, supporting her as she struggled to stay on her feet.

At the crisis passed, as her senses returned, Diana stepped out of her panties and sat on the edge of the huge white sofa pulling Ann down to sit beside her. They sat side by side, their stockinged thighs touching, the nylon rasping slightly.

Tex looked across at them wondering what was going to happen next, if that was the end or simply an intermission. He dare not speak for fear he said the wrong thing, in case something he said made them decide to stop.

'I came so hard,' Diana said to her friend, as though they were alone together.

'I know. I felt it,' Ann replied.

Very quietly Diana turned to her friend. She used the back of her hand to caress both her cheeks.

'You're so good . . . I love doing it with you.'

She kissed the cheeks where her hand had been. She kissed Ann's forehead, and her eyelids, delaying the moment that she kissed her mouth again. But Ann was only content to put up with such delicacies for a moment. She had her own needs.

175

Like a fire they were being stoked with fuel, the fuel of passion – by Diana's wonderful pliant body, by the two men sitting opposite them on the sofa, their faces set in expressions of total lust, by her own body as she looked down at herself, her powerful thighs bisected by the black welts of the stockings, the suspender straps loose on the top of her legs but stretched and taut at the sides.

Ann caught Diana's face in her hands and forced their mouths together. Her hot tongue plunged between Diana's lips and immediately both women felt a surge of unmitigated pleasure. Diana kissed back hard, sucking at Ann's tongue then pushing it aside with her own. With her hand she found Ann's breasts, the nipples hard as pebbles, and tweaked them in turn, pinching almost too hard, and feeling Ann's gasping response in her mouth. She repeated the process, pinching harder still, then using her palm to grind the nipple, one after the other, on to Ann's ribs. Ann moaned but the noise was gagged by Diana's tongue.

The initiative passed to Diana. She pushed Ann back on the sofa, right back and then twisted to the side, so Ann could draw her legs up – all this without breaking her kiss. As soon as Ann was lying flat Diana rolled on top of her, letting her fleshy tits press into Ann's chest, and grinding her pubis down on to the hard bone of Ann's pelvic triangle. Diana felt Ann's excitement as much as she felt her own: their bodies were tuned together, able to deliver harmonies to echo and amplify each other's feelings. Practice makes perfect.

What the men saw was an erotic spectacle they could hardly believe. Two gorgeous women, mouth on mouth, breasts squashed together, long legs intwined, their stockings pulled taut by the long thin black straps of the suspenders, a writhing mass of sex.

Diana was moving as if she had a cock, as if she were trying to fuck her friend with her tiny swollen clitoris. Ann opened her stockinged legs and bent her knees, bringing her legs up around Diana's arse, then up in the air further until her knees were only feet from her head. It opened her sex for Diana's thrust, angling her clitoris so it was directly under Diana's. They both felt it at the same moment, an sudden impact, clitoris on clitoris.

'Oh, my God . . .' Diana could not help herself from saying.

She thrust more gently, not wanting to lose the position, feeling the knot of Ann's nerves pulsing against her own.

Ann was coming. It was her turn. She could feel Diana's thrust right on the centre of her sexual being, feel Diana's heat and hardness. It was like a tiny cock. She wanted to open herself like a flower so Diana could penetrate her, fuck her. She felt herself blossoming, melting. Suddenly she bucked her hips up at Diana wanting no subtlety. Diana ground down on her, pushing her back, their clitorises rubbing together again pushed against the unyielding pubic bone.

'Oh, God . . .' Ann murmured, coming over Diana's clitoris or was it her own. They were so close she could not tell. It felt as though she had two clitorises and they were both bringing her off.

Diana moved only slightly, wanting to keep the precise contact, wetness on wetness, heat on heat.

She could feel Ann's orgasm as she had never felt it before. She hugged herself to her friend's body, her arms wrapped around her back, letting her feelings run their course, letting her wallow in delicious sensation.

But Diana was not content to leave it there. As soon as the tension in Ann's body subsided she rolled off her and got on to her knees. She had almost forgotten about the two men so engrossed had she been in her friend's pleasure. Now she looked up and saw them sitting, side by side, on the edge of the sofa opposite, their eyes full of wonder and lust and their own need. She could not see their erections but she was sure they were there, straining to escape the constriction of their clothes.

A shudder of pure pleasure gripped Diana's body like the tremor of orgasm. She watched the men watching her body convulse, her big breasts quivering.

Then she turned to Ann. She was kneeling at the side of Ann's hips facing her feet. She trailed her hand along Ann's thighs and up over her navel as if testing to see whether her body was ready for more. Ann moaned. She was ready. The extreme sensitivity that follows orgasm had passed. She was ready and more than willing. Diana brought her head down to her navel and licked her soft belly, running her tongue into Ann's sparse pubic hair. She moved her hands under Ann's open legs as her mouth slid down to the crease of Ann's sex and her tongue found her clitoris. With her hands under her buttocks, she licked the whole length of Ann's sex, from clitoris to anus, using the width of her tongue, letting Ann feel its roughness, long wet licks like a child licking an ice cream. Then she probed the entrance to her cunt. Straining her tongue forward Diana tasted Ann's copious juices, felt the tightness of her silky channel. She worked her hand round and replaced her tongue with her fingers. Two fingers then three crammed into the tight wet cunt, while her tongue sought out the clitoris again.

Ann's sex was soaked. The little puckered bud of her arse was slippery wet. Diana's fourth finger penetrated there almost by accident, following the movement of the other fingers and slipping into her anus naturally in all the liquid heat. Ann gasped at the intrusion.

Diana fucked her with her hand, feeling her whole sex wrapped around it, clinging, hot and throbbing. She moved her fingers in and out of her, while her mouth and tongue lapped at her clitoris.

But Ann wanted more. Struggling up from the sofa she caught hold of Diana's thigh and pulled. Diana knew what she wanted. Almost without breaking the rhythm she had established, Diana swung her thigh over Ann's face and lowered her hairy sex on to her friend's willing face.

In seconds Ann had impaled her fingers in Diana's cunt, her fourth finger in her anus, her mouth on her clitoris. They were a matched pair perfectly reflecting whatever one did to the other. Ann's rhythm was the same as Diana's. Diana probed deep with her fingers, so did Ann. Diana sucked harder on the thick swollen clitoris, so did Ann. Every feeling, every sensation, every shudder of uncontrollable passion was repeated, echoed, mirrored as the two women pressed their bodies into a perfect harmony.

They had felt this before. It had made them come before.

They were coming now and coming together. They both knew it though hardly consciously. Their bodies knew it. Their minds had long since given up the attempt to do anything but feel. Diana felt Ann's nipples at her navel, just as her own were pressed against Ann's hard flat belly. She felt her climax building, layer upon layer peeled away, her clitoris, her cunt, her whole body open and exposed. The more exposed the greater the feeling. She felt Ann's cunt begin to spasm, contracting violently, as her whole body trembled out of control. At the same moment her own cunt seemed to just melt over Ann's mouth in a vortex of thrilling sensation, her body quivering too.

Ann's fingers plunged deep into cunt and anus, the deepest they had been. Diana did the same. Both women knew it was their last action, the last thing they would be able to do before orgasm took over. And they were right. It was. Almost immediately, provoked perhaps by this final mutual penetration, their bodies heaved on waves of passion. It was an extraordinary feeling. They were so close, so intimate. Diana felt Ann's orgasm as much as she felt her own. Ann's orgasm took Diana higher, hotter, deeper and vice versa. The orgasms were doubled. As each went higher, the other felt it, experienced it, climbed higher too, hand over hand, feeding off each other's bodies until together they reached the final peak.

There was nothing but an all-embracing black-

ness. No sound, no feeling, just a thumping somewhere distant like a giant engine turning. It was a
long time before Diana realised the thumping was
her own heart.

Then she was aware of another sensation. She
was being lifted, her legs lifted physically off Ann's
face and to one side. Almost before she realised
what was happening, almost before she had moved
her head from between Ann's legs she felt her arse
being hoisted up and a hard hot cock nudging at
her labia to find her cunt. It did not have to search
for long. In seconds it was thrust inside her and
she could not help but gasp with pleasure. The cock
was hot. Red hot. She had never felt a cock so hot,
nor so excited. Its length, from tip to balls, seemed
to be pulsing, And it was ramming into her with an
urgency so great it literally took her breath away.

All this had happened so quickly she had not
opened her eyes from the euphoria of her orgasm.
Now as she blinked them open, she was startled to
see a cock in front of her, Tex's cock, as hard and
erect as the one reaming her cunt. Tex was naked,
his clothes abandoned. His big body, covered with a
mat of hair as thick as fur, was heavy with muscle.
He lowered himself between Ann's legs, to push his
cock deep into the soaking wetness of her cunt, a
wetness Diana had created.

Diana looked over her shoulder. John was naked
too. His hands held her hips as he fucked her, his
eyes closed as he pulled her back on to his cock,
his energy surging with lust, his whole being concentrated only on the need witnessing the incredible spectacle of these two women locked together
in orgasm, had created . . .

They had seen what they had seen. At first it

had been easy to watch, to appreciate the beauty
of the spectacle without being involved, to admire
and inspect without being drawn into the carnal
circle. But not for long. The mood had changed.
The performance had become too charged, too
involving, too provoking. It had not been possible
to sit back, to remain detached as though watching
some animated porno film, exciting but remote. Not
as they watched the two women ravishing each
other, their bodies synchronised in their passion, a
wild private passion. They had gone so far the men
had ceased to exist. It was no longer a game. Their
only consideration was their fulfilment.

Tex had looked at John Borland, a look of deadly
earnest. He was not smiling. They had not said a
word as they stripped off their clothes ...

John Borland was coming. He opened his eyes.
In front of him he saw Ann's big body being battered by Tex, watched as Tex's penis slid in and out
of her cunt, shining and slippery with her juices,
watched as his hands kneaded her tits, pinched
her nipples, as Ann's long stockinged legs wrapped
around Tex's back, her heels digging into his flesh
as she urged him on. He saw his own cock plunging
into Diana's cunt at the bottom of the deep cleft of
her arse, her long back laid out in front of him, the
thin black suspender belt dividing it in two.

Ann's eyes were open too. As Tex powered into
her she could see John's cock taking Diana, see his
big hairy balls banging against her labia. She knew
what Diana was feeling. Their feelings were perfectly matched again. After what they had done
together, she had felt an urgent need for cock. It
had been the same after every experience they had

shared together. Woman on woman was wonderful, tender, strong, orgasmic. But they were not lesbian. They needed cock. Craved for it.

They had got exactly what they needed.

Diana reached out with her hand and ran it over Tex's thigh. With an effort she insinuated it down over his arse. If this was a sexual tryst, a *ménage à quatre*, she wanted it to be complete.

'Yes, baby, yes . . .' Tex cried. He wanted it too.

Ann looked down to see what he meant. She saw Diana's arm and understood immediately. She reached up over her shoulder groping for John's thigh. She understood. The four bodies were to be joined, linked, the circle complete.

Diana's finger found Tex's anus. She penetrated it and heard him moan. He stopped pumping into Ann and let Diana thrust in and out of him. Ann's hand slid over John's buttock, felt the cleft of his arse, felt blindly for his anus, found it, thrust inside it, plunged in and out.

A perfect circle. The four members pierced, hoisted on a human petard, cock or finger. Four bodies combined, bound together, connected, a Gordian knot of sex. For a moment they did not move. By unspoken consent they waited, wanting to remember what it felt like, every detail, every crevice of feeling in the sensation that none of them had ever experienced before.

Diana broke the spell. She moved her hand from Tex's arse down to his balls. They were hairy and wet, slippery with Ann's copious juices. But Diana reeled them in, his scrotum her net, until she cupped them both in her palm.

'Yes ... yes ...' Tex shouted, resuming his thrusts.

Ann did the same. She groped and found John's balls. She squeezed them, kneaded them, milked them. Milked them of their sperm. She could feel Diana's cunt radiating heat above her hand.

Still cupping his balls in her palm Diana's fingers extended up along the shaft of Tex's cock until her middle finger was at the lips of Ann's cunt, then passed the lips into the cunt itself, driven there by Tex's thrusts. For him that was the last straw, he could hold back no longer. It was beyond his endurance. He was even surprised he had managed to hold on this long. To have seen what he had seen, to have fucked Ann's eager cunt would have been enough for most men. But this, another woman squeezing his balls, putting her finger alongside his cock ...

Diana felt his cock begin to spasm, felt him buck one last time unable to hold back any longer, and then felt his spunk pumping out, exploding out into Ann's consuming, open cunt.

John was not far behind. Ann's hand on his balls had taken him over the edge too. His mind was full of images of female flesh, long legs sheathed in sheer black nylon, stretched taut suspenders, cunt on cunt, tits and pliant flesh pressed together, as he felt his balls squeezed in one woman's hand while he fucked another. He thrust and thrust, not pausing to wait for his cock to spasm, but driving on, not stopping at all until every last drop of spunk had wrung itself from his rigid cock.

Tex was the first to move. 'I need a drink,' he declared, the words rousing them all from a trance-like reverie. Getting up from the sofa he walked over to the Armagnac bottle, poured himself a large measure and drunk it down in one gulp. He held the bottle aloft. 'Anyone else?' he asked.

They all accepted, dragging themselves into sitting positions and reaching for the glasses in turn.

'I never felt more like a drink in my life,' Ann said seriously.

'Quite a performance . . .' John muttered, sipping the smooth liquid.

'You can say that again,' Tex said, more forcefully.

Diana felt the warmth of the brandy spreading through her, steadying her body which was still trembling as though in mild shock. Not that the sensation was unpleasant. It wasn't. She felt relaxed and comfortable. She felt good. Very good. The trembling was her body's reaction to overstimulation not her mind's. In general, she thought to herself, she felt euphoric. Another step had been taken, another bridge crossed, another landmark on the sexual odyssey she had embarked on since The Event. But if she were honest with herself, that was not all she was feeling. Somewhere deep inside her there was another feeling, another motor running. At the moment it was idling, just a pleasant trill, the slightest of vibrations, but there sure enough. She knew precisely what it was and what it meant.

Diana got to her feet, unclipped the stockings and pulled them off her legs. She reached down behind her back and unhooked the suspender belt letting it fall to the floor. She was aware of both men watching her slow precise movements.

'Where's the bathroom?' she asked Tex.

'There's one off the master bedroom, babe...' he indicated the corridor behind them. 'Second on the left...'

'Show me,' she said, in a tone that would brook no argument.

'Sure thing, babe,' Tex said, only mildly taken aback.

Naked, he lead the way across the room and down a long corridor carpeted in thick cream wool and in which a Hockney oil hung, lit by carefully arranged concealed lighting. He opened one of a pair of walnut-panelled doors into the main bedroom. The walls were covered in tan leather, the floor was the same cream wool as the hall. The large king-sized bed was draped with a fur counterpane.

'Through there...' he said, showing her a wall that was entirely covered in mirrors. It took Diana a moment to realise that one of the mirrored panels was inset with a small brass handle.

Instead of setting off across the room Diana turned to Tex. With both of her hands she lifted her tits, as though trying to gauge what weight they were.

'Do you like my tits?' she said, using the word 'tits' deliberately, wanting to sound crude.

'They're great...' He was staring at them.

'Good. I like your body.'

'It's OK, I guess... Listen I thought...'

'What?'

'You were with John?'

She couldn't suppress a laugh. 'After what we've just done isn't that irrelevant?'

'Guess so . . .'

'I want you, Tex.' That was the motor running in her body. That was her need. She squeezed the great mounds of her breasts. 'Do you want me?'

'You bet, babe . . .'

She saw his cock swell slightly.

'Go and get the others. Bring them in here.' Again her tone left no room for argument.

Diana let go of her breasts and walked into the bathroom. Her body was alive with anticipation again. This was the new Diana Wilson, the wild wanton self-fulfilling Diana Wilson. It was in the end her own directness, her own capacity to get precisely what she wanted with no inhibitions, no must or must nots, that, she knew, excited her most. She had seen Tex fucking Ann in front of her eyes and she wanted him to fuck her too. It was as simple as that. Ask and ye shall be given . . .

The bathroom was black marble. She stared at her reflection in the long mirror. She was smiling. Her face looked unconcerned, untroubled, innocent even. It reflected little of the passion that was churning in her body.

She peed, then used the bidet to wash her sex. From the bathroom cabinet, seemingly equipped with every female as well as male need, she took a jar of cold cream.

Back in the bedroom the fur counterpane had been thrown off the bed. John lay on the bed on his back. Ann was kneeling between his open legs, his cock buried in her mouth. Diana was not surprised. Ann had clearly suffered the same longings in relation to John as Diana had felt for Tex.

Perhaps, *ménage à quatre* it was ever thus.

'Quite a picture,' Diana said.

Tex lay beside them on the bed. Ann still wore her sheer black stockings, now the only clothing in a sea of nakedness.

'You don't mind?' John asked, though there was no real concern in his voice that she might.

'Tex is going to fuck me,' Diana said. The words increased the level of her excitement.

John made no reply. Ann's mouth on his cock suddenly demanded all his attention.

Diana came up to the bed and stroked the long curve of Ann's buttock. Then she got up onto the bed and knelt between Tex's legs. She reached down with her hands and wanked his already semi-erect cock. She felt it swell immediately. The she lent forward and nestled it between her breasts. She wriggled her breasts from side to side slapping his cock to and fro. Tex moaned, fully erect now.

Diana mounted him. She moved her thighs over his hips until her labia were poised above his cock. Tex's hands seized her tits, weighing them in his hands as though he couldn't believe his luck.

'You're some broad . . .' he said.

'Fuck me then,' was Diana's response. Feeling behind her to position his cock in the channel of her cunt, then sinking down on it, and feeling it slide effortlessly into her wet sex. 'Fuck me . . .'

Tex bucked his hips off the bed, his cock as hard as a bone as he felt Diana's cunt wrapping itself around him. He had never felt more turned on in his life. He looked over to see Ann's short brunette hair bobbing up and down as she worked on the long stem of John's cock, her lips pursed around it, her mouth taking most of its length right down into the back of her throat. He looked up at Diana's body, his hands on her tits, her face slack with passion. He drove into her, his cock reacting to the images all around him.

But Diana was not content yet. She wanted more and she intended to get it.

'Ann...' she said. Ann stopped pumping on John's cock. 'Ann, I want him too.' Diana's voice was calm, belying her intense excitement.

Ann's eyes focused on the jar of cold cream Diana had dropped on the bed between the two men. Then she looked into Diana's eyes. There was an unspoken dialogue. ('Is it really what you want?' 'Yes.' 'Do you think you can take it?' 'You bet.')

There was nothing else to be said. Ann had seen that look of determination in her friend's eyes before. She reached for the jar, opened it and smeared John's cock with the thick white cream. It was as if the men did not matter, they had no opinion, they were there only to do as they were told. John looked into Diana's face. She did not smile at him.

'What's going on?' Tex said.

'Shut up,' Diana told him.

Ann was pulling John up. She got him to his knees. It was important somehow that she manoeuvred him, that he did not do it unassisted.

'You know what I want,' Diana said.

'I've never done it before.'

'Do it for me.' She lent forward. Tex had released her breasts and they swung gently in front of her, their nipples grazing his hairy chest. He had as much hair as John. More perhaps. His cock was still deep inside her.

John positioned himself behind their bodies,

directed and coaxed into place by Ann. Diana felt his erection in the small of her back. She lent forward further still. Tex levered his head up to kiss her mouth, pushing his tongue between her lips, another intrusion into her body. Ann was caressing the tight curve of her buttock, her finger searching for the little corona of her anus. It found its objective and, white with cold cream where Ann had plunged it into the jar, now plunged deep into Diana's tight dark passage. Diana gasped, her mouth suddenly slack on Tex's lips, unable to concentrate on the kissing too as Ann's finger explored, creaming her arse as it went.

Ann could feel the hard bone of Tex's cock only separated from her finger by a thin layer of inner membrane. She felt it react as she moved along its length. She felt Diana react too, her body trembling with pleasure.

Reluctantly Ann withdrew her finger. She took John's cock in her hand and positioned it where her finger had explored. He hesitated.

Diana wriggled back on the hard hot cock nestling between the cheeks of her arse, wanting it inside her, wanting it alongside the other cock, wanting to feel for the first time in her life, her body filled with cock.

'Do it,' she cried, 'do it.'

Ann prodded him forward, pushing his buttocks. The cream on his cock and the preparation of Ann's finger made penetration easy. His cock slid into the tight passage up to the hilt.

Up until this point Diana had been in control. She had been the ring master of this particular circus. No longer. Something snapped in both men.

Any desire to hold back, to be gentle, to be considerate, died with the reality of the feeling of being inside this woman together, one by one, hot and wet and hard.

They started a rhythm. No subtlety. No deft strokes. Just hard and furious, taking what they could get. In and out like a power hammer. Tex bucking up into her cunt and out as John thrust into her arse. A perfect rhythm. In and out. Synchronised. It had to be. There was no room for mistakes. The feelings multiplied.

There was pain but only pain of intense, feverish pleasure.

Diana had come on Ann's finger. She had come as John's cock sunk into her arse. She had come as Tex had pushed up alongside him in her cunt again. She came again as Ann cupped her breasts and pinched her nipples. There seemed to be nothing but body-wretching sensation. She managed to wrest her eyes open for no more that a second to look down at Tex, to look down between her legs, her hairy pubis framing Tex's cock as it plunged in and out of her. She thought she could see John's cock too but, of course, she could not. In her mind she saw it. As another orgasm (or was it just one long orgasm rattling around in her body like a penny in a glass?) forced her eyes closed, in the blackness she could see both cocks sawing back and forth, one on top of the other, using the passages of her body, filling her, fucking her, taking her. It was what she'd wanted.

Tex was going to spunk first. Diana sensed it. His cock was hammering faster and faster. She used her cunt muscles to squeeze it and immediately felt her body contract on two cocks not just one. It made her come. And her shuddering gasping body was all that Tex could take. He bucked up one more time, then back slightly, finding his place. In the wet caverns of her cunt, against her silky dark walls, invaded by another monster too, his cock spasmed and spat his hot white gobs of spunk into the space he had found.

John felt it. He felt Diana's orgasm. Her whole body was trembling. She was making little mewing noises like an animal. Her long fair hair hung down from her shoulders, her heavy tits quivering. He continued to plunge forward. There was no way he could control himself even if he'd wanted to. His cock was too full of spunk again, and his mind too full of unbelievable images of sex.

Ann held Diana's breast in her hand, kneading it, pulling it, nipping at the nipple. With her other hand she trailed her fingers across John's mouth. He sucked on them eagerly. Then she rolled them away and found his nipple. With the fingernail of her thumb and forefinger she pinched it, making crescents in the tender flesh. She repeated the process on the other nipple.

That took him over the top. The pain she inflicted turned immediately to fiery pleasure. The tightness around his cock, tighter that her cunt, seemed to suck him in, closing around him, hot and creamed. His mind was telling him what he was doing, what he had done, a voice repeating it over and over in his head. He felt and saw everything he had done that night. It all seemed to coalesce suddenly. He opened his eyes and looked down at his cock reaming into the cleft between Diana's magnificent pert buttocks and he came, his cock still powering forward as his spunk jetted out into Diana's arse.

Diana thought she had come enough, that she was finished, but her body had other ideas. As she felt his cock twitching inside her, depositing his load, swelling, stretching her passage even more, she came. Like the final wave of the ebb tide, she felt herself dragged down and down and down, across the sand and pebbles and shells, each one scratching and pricking her body, before she was gathered up in a huge torrent of water. Gathered up until she was surfing, flying higher and higher on the crest of a wave, so high she thought she would never come down, then crashing vertically on to the unyielding shore in an explosion of foam and sand and emotion, so suddenly she had no breath, no being, nothing but sensation.

They lay on the bed at different angles to each other, limbs crossing limbs, a tangle of bodies like some sculpture of an ancient Indian god. It was hard to tell which arm belonged to which body. Exhaustion prevented movement.

Eventually John disentangled himself and went back into the living room. He returned with the Armagnac and a brandy balloon. He poured a large measure into the glass and passed it around.

'Well, you girls are going to have to come to Texas. That's for sure. I'll send my plane for you, is it a deal?'

'Any time,' Diana said, her body too awash with feeling to say anything else.

'Just one thing,' Ann said, looking at the two flaccid cocks.

'What's that, baby?' Tex asked.

'Aren't I going to get my turn?' Ann pouted like a little girl who'd missed out on a slice of birthday cake.

They all laughed.

'Poor Ann ... I'm sure you can come up with something can't you?' Diana said, looking at the two men in turn.

And, eventually they did.

Chapter Eight

'Diana, it's Maggie.'

It was ten o'clock in the morning and Diana was sitting in the kitchen reading the newspaper and finishing a pot of coffee.

'Hi, Maggie. How's business?'

'The usual. Are you available this afternoon?'

'Of course.'

'It's one of Carolyn's oldest clients. George Adams.'

'How old?'

'I don't mean age. I mean he's been with us since the beginning.'

'A regular.'

'Right. He's also very rich. Seriously rich.'

Diana could see Maggie's small features, almost rat-like, as she listened. No doubt she was sitting in the office in her usual twin set and pearls. Her young energetic voice did not match her appearance at all. The men who phoned would be beguiled into thinking Maggie was some young voluptuous creature, not a middle-aged spinster with horn-rimmed spectacles.

'So, what do I have to do?' she asked.

* * *

Three hours later Diana Wilson was dressed to the nines, made-up, and standing outside the main entrance to Harrods looking for the white Jaguar saloon that was to meet her. It was exactly on time. The car glided up to the curb, the chauffeur raced round to the rear door and opened it, and Diana climbed into the back seat, making herself comfortable in the grey leather as the chauffeur ran round again and got behind the wheel.

'How long will it take?' Diana asked.

'No more than an hour, madam,' the chauffeur replied, pulling the car out into the Knightsbridge traffic.

They drove west. The chauffeur volunteered no further information and Diana asked for none. She wondered if he knew who she was and why she was being taken to the house. He was tall and skinny, so tall his chauffeur's cap grazed the roof lining of the car. He was young too, no more than twenty-five Diana guessed. In the rear-view mirror Diana could see his light blue eyes. Occasionally, as he checked the traffic, they lighted on her. She had opened her coat and the skirt of the black dress she was wearing revealed some inches above her knees.

He drove precisely, with the minimum of effort, his black leather gloved hands gliding over the wheel as though caressing it, as though it were something alive.

Diana felt a frisson of lust. It was three days since what, she thought, could properly be described as her orgy with Tex and John. Since then her body had told her it needed a rest. She was sore and satiated. Neither her mind nor her body had responded to sexual stimulus. Now, it appeared, she had made a recovery. As well as the obvious attractions of the chauffeur she felt the thrill of anticipation again as the car sped her to another assignation, another page of sexual adventure.

Perhaps it was the excitement of the prospect that lay ahead but Diana found it difficult to ignore the chauffeur's charms.

'You're very tall aren't you?'

'Yes, madam,' he said curtly, as if to end further questions.

'How tall?'

'Six four.'

'How long have you been working for Mr Adams?'

'Two years, madam.'

'Is he a good employer?'

'Yes, madam.'

'Do you like driving?'

'Yes, madam.'

Diana gave up the attempt to make conversation. The monosyllabic responses clearly indicated the chauffeur did not want to chat, or was under instructions not to.

They left the suburbs of London and the winding country lanes of Buckinghamshire took over.

After a little more than an hour the car drove through a pair of ornate wrought iron gates and up a long winding driveway to the front of a large mansion house. The house was enormous by any standards. Diana imagined, from the clusters of herring-boned brick chimneys, that it was originally Elizabethan, but successive generations had added and subtracted to it, imposing their own styles, so the basic building was now fronted by a

Georgian façade and a large wing had been added which owed its Gothic grandeur to the Victorians. The house was obviously set in extensive grounds. Several expensive cars, Aston Martin, Ferrari, Lotus, were parked in an area to the right of the main buildings, largely surrounded by tall shrubs.

The Jaguar drove right up to the front door which was opened by a woman the moment the car came to rest. She was obviously elderly but walked with no infirmity, her back ramrod straight. She wore a simple maid's uniform of black skirt, black lisle stockings and crisp white blouse.

The chauffeur opened the rear door of the car. He was given a good view of Diana's legs as she climbed from the car and clearly took advantage of it. For the first time Diana felt he was not as oblivious to her as he'd pretended.

'This way,' the woman said, with more than a little impatience.

Diana followed the woman into the house. Immediately, she could hear the muffled sound of voices, laughter, cutlery and crockery, coming from somewhere inside. A large lunch party was in progress. The elderly woman led the way down a long hall, carpeted in the centre but with oak floorboards at the sides, until they reached a small wood-panelled door. She opened it.

'You understand what is required of you?' she said brusquely.

'I think so.'

Maggie had explained. It was apparently the same every year.

Diana walked into the room and the housekeeper, if that's what she was, snapped the door closed, leaving her alone. The room had no decorations and no furniture save a single straight-backed wooden chair that looked as though it had been bought at a jumble sale. It had no window either, the only light came from a naked light-bulb hanging from a wire in the middle of the ceiling. Having been told by Maggie exactly what to expect, she was not surprised to find a long black cloak hanging from a hook on the back of the door. She slipped out of her dress and her bra and panties. She had put on a pair of black hold-up stockings, their tops patterned with black lace. She wasn't sure whether she should take them off too. For the time being she decided to leave them on.

Just as she plucked the cloak from the back of the door it was opened slowly. It was not the housekeeper. A man in his sixties wearing evening dress with a black bow-tie shuffled into the room rather uneasily. From his manner it was clear he had been drinking quite a lot of alcohol. The man was fat. He was not tall and his cummerbund encompassed a considerable paunch. His cheeks, ruddy with drink, were round and chubby. His chin and jowls hung down on this throat in multiple layers, right the way down to the collar of his white shirt.

'Hello, there,' he said, slurring his words.

'Mr Adams?' Diana asked.

'Well, you are a real beauty. A real beauty.' He rifled in his pocket and came out with a sealed plastic packet of notes, obviously straight from the bank. It was a thousand-pound bundle of fifty-pound notes. As he handed it to Diana they dropped out of his hand. He scrambled on the floor to pick them up, almost falling over in the process.

He straightened up, his face now redder than ever, and gave Diana the money. She put it in her bag without a word, though Maggie had given her no indication she would be paid that much.

'Do you mind?' he said, indicating the cloak which she was holding in such a way as to obscure his view of her body.

At these prices, she thought, you can be my guest. She put the cloak down on the chair. 'I was going to ask if I should wear these stockings? I know you specify naked?'

For a moment he said nothing, his eyes riveted to the triangle of thick fair pubic hair, almost as though he couldn't believe it was real. 'Oh yes, I think you look very nice like that. Very nice indeed.'

He was obviously telling the truth. Diana could see a bulge developing under his fly.

'I'm afraid I've had a drink or two,' he said.

'Really?' Diana said, trying to keep sarcasm out of her voice.

'Yes . . . well it's a party you see.'

'So I understand . . .'

'I wouldn't ask normally . . . but you are very nice . . .'

'Ask away?'

'I don't suppose . . .' He rifled through his pockets again and came out with more fifty-pound notes, these were loose. Five or six fell to the floor. He did not stoop to pick them up this time.

'What exactly do you want?'

'It's against the rules. You mustn't tell.'

'My lips are sealed.'

'Just . . .' The explanation appeared to be difficult

for him. Instead Adams took her hand and placed it on the front of his trousers. 'Such lovely legs ... the thighs, so straight ... and all that hair ...'

Diana found the top of the zip under the cummerbund. Pulling it down, she knelt in front of him. He swayed slightly and put his hand out against the wall to steady himself. She fished in his fly. A pair of boxer shorts parted to allow her fingers to feel soft fat flesh. To one side she felt his erection. Circling it with her hand she began to pull it out. But before she could get it clear of his clothing she suddenly felt it pulse violently and a wet warmth spread over her hand and the cotton of the boxer shorts. He'd spunked at the first touch of her cool fingers. A damp stain spread across the front of his trousers.

He pulled her hand away and zipped himself up.

'Wonderful,' he mumbled. 'Wonderful. Such lovely legs. Such a nice touch. Wonderful. I'll send the housekeeper for you when we're ready ... won't be long. Wonderful ...' And George Adams was gone, the money still lying on the floor.

By the time Diana had salted the money away in her bag, wondered if two hundred and fifty pounds for ten seconds was some sort of record, and debated whether she should put the cloak on, the housekeeper returned, still not in a mood to venture a smile.

'Put this on,' she said, holding out what looked like a crumpled piece of highly coloured rubber. In fact it was a rubber mask, the sort moulded to resemble the faces of the famous. This one was an effigy of Margaret Thatcher. Diana pulled it over her head. She adjusted it to fit her eyes. There was no opening for her mouth.

'Hands behind your back, please,' the house-keeper ordered.

'What for?' Diana's voice was muffled by the rubber mask.

'They have to be bound,' she said, in a tone that suggested Diana must be educationally subnormal for not knowing something so obvious.

Diana did not argue. Maggie had omitted this detail but it was too late now to object. Besides Diana's curiosity was aroused and with it her omnivorous sexuality.

The housekeeper took a strip of velvet and expertly bound Diana's wrists together. Just as efficiently, she bound another strip of velvet around Diana's elbows just above the joint. This had the effect of forcing Diana's chest forward, making her back straight and her breasts even more promi-nent. Picking up the cloak from the chair the woman clipped it around Diana's neck, adjusting it until she was satisfied it hung evenly all round. Finally, she fastened a small leather strap over the collar of the cloak. Attached to the leather was a short metal leash which fell between the folds of the cloak, the metal cold as it rested between Diana's breasts.

'Wait here,' the housekeeper ordered and closed the door sharply behind her.

It was hot under the rubber mask. Diana sat down sideways on the chair, her arms aching already from their bondage. The cloak fell open and she looked down at her breasts, the cold metal chain hanging between them, her nipples corru-gated and hard. The chain pooled in her lap. She opened her legs and it fell down against her labia. It made her shudder.

She remembered this feeling of bondage. She remembered Julie. She flushed with excitement. She closed her legs on the chain and squeezed her thighs together. She knew if she could have touched herself she would have been wet. The chain bit into her soft flesh. Why was it so exciting to be deprived of the ability to touch? Though she knew it was useless, she struggled against the bindings – as she had struggled on Julie's bed tied and spread – so she would feel the constriction. It thrilled her, as it had before. She squeezed her thighs together again and the chain moved deeper into her labia, insinuating itself, the links resting against her clitoris now. A flood of feeling was the consequence. She closed her eyes. Almost an orgasm.

It was all so strange. Tied up here in this tiny room. Available. Open. The cold chain pressed into her sex. Her body shuddered again. She tensed the muscles of her thighs . . .

'This way,' the housekeeper barked, opening the door but not coming in, making Diana start.

Diana got to her feet a little unsteadily with no balance from her arms. She didn't want the housekeeper to see what had happened to the chain.

As soon as they were outside the room the housekeeper picked up the end of the leash and led Diana along the corridor by it. If it was wet she gave no indication.

They approached a large pair of intricately panelled oak doors. Diana could hear the noise of conversation on the other side. The housekeeper knocked loudly twice on the door. The rumble of conversation died away to be replaced by a single voice. Diana could not hear what was said.

The door was opened from the inside by George Adams. He appeared a little steadier on his feet. Taking the leash from the housekeeper's hand he led Diana into the room.

'Gentlemen, a prize I think you will all agree, worthy of the occasion.'

Sitting around a large dining table bedecked with flowers and silver candelabrum and the debris of what had obviously been an elaborate and extensive meal, were twelve men all in evening dress. On one side of the room a large fireplace was filled with a crackling log fire, on the other, a wall of leaded windows overlooked the picturesque garden.

Diana was led round the table. With her hands tied behind her back she could not prevent the cloak from opening as she moved to reveal tantalising glimpses of her naked body. Her high heels clacked on the wooden floor. The man's eyes followed her procession. There were muttered comments. ('Look at those tits', 'Tight little arse', 'So much hair'.) When they had completed the journey Adams dropped into his chair at the head of the table, as if he had just completed a six mile route march, leaving Diana standing at his side. Margaret Thatcher's face stared at the men unsmiling.

'Well, gentlemen, you all know the rules by now...'

In front of him the housekeeper had placed a dark blue velvet bag pulled tight at its neck by a silk plaited draw-string. He undid the string just enough to allow a hand into the bag then knotted it again. He passed the bag to the man on his right.

'Fifty numbers. Twelve of you. Lowest number drawn wins . . .'

The first man fumbled with the bag nervously. Before he put his hand in he looked up at Diana. The expression of lust in his face betrayed no subtlety. He groped in the velvet and withdrew a bright red ball the size of a golf-ball and inscribed with the number twenty-five. His face dissolved in disappointment. He passed the bag to the man on his left, who shook the bag vigorously and withdrew the number twenty-nine.

'My usual luck . . .' he said passing the bag on.

At the sixth attempt a cry went up from the far end of the table.

'Three. You've got three to beat.'

Diana looked at the man who had jumped to his feet in delight. He was short, fat and bald with the sort of skin that seemed to exude grease. His eyes were small and piggy. He regarded Diana proprietorially, as if she was already his.

The bag continued its progress. 'Nine', 'Eleven', 'Thirty-one' and 'Twenty-one' were called out. There were two men left. Diana watched as the bag was passed along. The second from last man was young, the youngest at the table and also looked the least affected by alcohol. In fact he had a bottle of Perrier on the table in front of him and his wine glass was full of red wine. He fumbled in the bag. There were lots of balls left.

He drew a ball out, looked at it and put it down on the white linen cloth without saying anything.

For some reason Diana did not understand, he looked disgusted with himself. The man next to him snatched the ball up.

'Two, he's got two, Albie,' he shouted to the man who'd drawn the three.

'It's a fix.'

'My turn,' the man said. Quickly he plunged his hand in and drew out a red ball. 'Thirty-three. I knew it. I've never bloody won in ten years.'

'We have a winner,' Adams declared solemnly. 'Will you please unmask your prize.'

The winner stood up with great reluctance, came over to Diana and took hold of the rubber mask.

'Is she a beauty, is she a beast...' Adams intoned, the rest of the table joining in – 'has the winner won the one he wants least?'

The rubber mask was pulled off. Diana shook her hair out and looked into the eyes of the man who had won.

'Beauty!' Came a chorus of voices from around the table.

The winner did not look into Diana's eyes. He picked up the chain leash with about as much enthusiasm as if it were attached to a rabid dog and led her out of the room. A tattoo of handclapping began in time to her steps accompanied by a chorus of obscenities ('Fuck that little arse', 'Give her one for me'). Most of the men got up from the table and followed them into the corridor, like a pack of baying hounds and making just as much noise.

Breaking into a trot the winner led her up an elaborately carved wooden staircase, down a short hallway and into a small bedroom quickly closing the door against the rabble who had followed on their heels.

Immediately the door was shut, the man came over to Diana and unstrapped the collar that held the leash. They could hear the men outside talking excitedly as they made their way down-stairs again.

Though the bedroom was small, it was beauti-fully furnished, its curtains, carpets and counter-pane all co-ordinated in various shades of pink. On an antique chest of drawers was a bottle of Cognac and two glasses.

'I had to bring you up here. Sorry. I'm really sorry.' He still did not look into her eyes.

'What are you sorry for?'

'For all this. I hate it. I have to take part. It's like a company institution. If you don't take part well ... I've never won before.'

'And now you have.'

'We wait half-an-hour and that's that.' He took a cigarette case from his pocket, snapped it open and lit a cigarette with a gold Cartier lighter.

'What's your name?'

'Phil.'

Phil was no more than thirty. He was short, even a little shorter that Diana in her heels. His hair was fair and neatly styled. His eyes, worried now, his brow creased, were a deep sea-green. Under the cummerbund of the evening suit a small paunch had developed but, as yet, it was not out of control.

'Oh, I'm sorry ... let me untie you,' he said look-ing at her awkward posture.

'Take the cloak off first,' Diana said calmly.

'Sorry?'

'You heard.'

He put the cigarette down and looked puzzled. He fumbled with the fastening of the cloak. It fell to the floor. He did not look at her body.

'I'll untie you.'

Perhaps he imagined the cloak had to be removed to get to her bonds.

'And if I don't want to be untied?'

'I don't understand... This whole thing's so awful...'

'I know it's awful. I appreciate your sensitivity. But I have feelings too...'

'That's exactly what I...'

'And my feelings are aroused. Very aroused. Do you know what it feels like to be paraded like that? Naked, except for that cloak. Not able to keep it from parting. Paraded around in front of all those leering eyes. All wanting me. Lusting for me. Do you think I'd have agreed to it just for the money? The money's nothing to do with it. It was a turn-on. Do you know what it feels like now, to be here with you, tied like this?'

'No...' he said, swallowing hard.

'It excites me. Does that shock you? If I told you I wanted to be fucked, needed it, would you be shocked? As a matter of fact if you're not going to fuck me I'd rather you went and got someone who will.'

The look of astonishment on the man's face did not last for long. It changed in seconds to an altogether different reaction. His eyes looked at Diana's naked body for the first time, her heavy plump breasts thrust forward by her pinioned arms, her thick thatch of pubic hair, her long thighs, banded in the middle by the black lace of the hold-up stockings, her high heels pointing her foot at a sharp angle.

'You want it . . .' It was not a question. It was a realisation. He could see it in her eyes.

'Yes. Do you want me to say please?' she said sarcastically.

It was all true, everything she had told him. Diana was as turned on as she'd been with most of her bizarre recent experiences.

It had started in the small bare room downstairs, the cold chain pressed into her sex, the sudden memories of Julie. But the arousal she had felt, led round the table of men, watching their eyes, knowing their thoughts had been something else, a new excitement. The key, the central nodule of her feelings, was that she had chosen to be there. She had put herself into this situation. It was how she lived now. And she loved it.

She could feel her wetness seeping out from her body.

Phil was stripping off his clothes like a whirling dervish. When he turned to face her, naked, his cock was erect. It was circumcised and large, its glans bulbous and out of proportion to the rest of his cock.

Diana sat on the bed then scrambled herself back until she was in the middle of the sheets. With her arms tied as they were she was already arched up, her cunt angled towards him. She opened her legs wide, as wide as they would go.

He stood at the foot of the bed looking into her sex as though it were some exotic animal he had never seen before.

Climbing on to the bed between her legs he gripped her ankles in his hands and raised her legs into the air until they formed a massive V. Slowly he closed them until her ankles were together. He pushed forward moving his grip down to the back of her knees until her legs were doubled up on her body, her thighs pressing into her breasts, her knees almost under her chin. Positioned like this the whole of Diana's sex was exposed, from the little barnacle of her anus to the thick mouth of her labia, fleshy and wrinkled and already wet with excitement.

He pulled himself towards her and with no ceremony stuck his cock into her cunt. It was soaking wet. As soon as he felt her wetness, as if needing that confirmation, he rammed himself in to the hilt. His hands held her legs down on top of her. He looked down at the apex of her sex. In this position he could see his cock thrusting in and out of her cunt, see the whole long crease of her labia stretched around his stem, pursed around it. It looked like a mouth puckered in a kiss.

He managed to hold both her legs down with one hand bridged across the back of her knees. The other hand he used to find her clitoris. It was already exposed. Using his fingers he strummed it as if it were the string of some strange instrument. He watched himself doing it.

Diana moaned. She was coming, coming on the idea of helplessness, coming on the feeling of her arms bound behind her, legs forced into the air, her cunt invaded, her clitoris wanked so unceremoniously. She was panting for breath, doubled-up as she was all her weight rested on her arms

and all his weight too. His cock felt hot and deep.
She knew he was going to spunk quickly, she could
feel his cock swelling. But she came first. A long
thin stab of pleasure sliced into her body, hot and
black and electric and she felt her cunt contract
around this stranger. She struggled against her
bonds, not to escape but involuntarily as her
muscles locked and her nerves were overwhelmed
by breathless sensation.

He could see her come. He could see the lips of
her sex contracting around him, spasming, like the
mouth of a fish out of water. He could feel it too,
squeezing his cock, making him come. He came
with his eyes open, watching as the sword of flesh
was swallowed down into her glistening wet
depths.

'You needed that,' he said.

He lowered her legs. She rolled over on to her
back. Her arms ached now from their bondage.

'Didn't you believe me?'

He worked on the velvet knots until she was free.

'I thought it was what you were supposed to say.
Part of the act. To get me to perform. But it wasn't,
was it?'

'No. I wanted it.'

And, of course, that was the simple truth.

The Jaguar swung up to the front door, the chauffeur got out and ran round to open the rear door
and Diana, escorted out of the mansion by the
housekeeper, climbed into the back seat. George
Adams would have liked to have thanked her personally she was told, but unfortunately he was
indisposed.

Diana felt coquettish. The experience of being raffled, of being the first prize in some annual corporate event, had been something she was unlikely to forget. But she had been disappointed when the winner of the prize had shown no inclination to continue after he had taken her the first time. In fact he had appeared embarrassed as though regretting he had been tempted at all and had scurried out of the room as soon as he was dressed, not looking at her again nor saying a word.

It had left Diana feeling far from satisfied. The residue of excitement sung in her body, a resonance she could feel in all her nerves. Sitting back in the leather of the Jaguar Diana's attention turned to the driver once again.

'Do you do this every year? It's an annual event isn't it?'

'Yes,' he said. The same monosyllabic response.

'You're not very chatty are you?'

'No, madam,' he said.

'You know you're a very attractive man. I find you very attractive.'

He said nothing.

'So, once a year Mr Adams has you come to town to pick up a woman to be the first prize in his raffle.'

'Raffle?'

'Didn't you know?'

'What raffle?' he asked angrily, as though she must be talking nonsense.

'It's an annual event. Encouragement for corporate executives. What did you think was going on? All those men and one woman?'

'I'm not paid to think.'

212

But Diana could see thinking was precisely what he was doing now. At least Diana had got some reaction. She wanted more. She wanted to provoke him. His control, his silence was a challenge.

Diana put her foot on to the transmission tunnel that ran down the centre of the car, bending her knee and opening her legs. Her skirt rode up over her thighs.

'What they do . . . They had me take off all my clothes, except my stockings. I was allowed to keep my stockings on. And my high heels. Then I was bound. What's your name?'

'Patrick,' he said trying not to look in the rear-view mirror.

'The housekeeper bound my arms, Patrick. Behind my back. It was a strange feeling. Can you imagine? Not being able to touch yourself. When someone deprives you of the ability to do something you instantly want to do it, don't you? Imperative. I wanted so badly to touch my nipples . . .'

Diana's intention was to excite the driver, but she was exciting herself. She ran her hand up the black nylon of her leg and on to the crotch of her panties. She pressed it into her labia and could not stop a moan of pleasure. They were tender from her earlier encounter.

She looked into the rear-view mirror. The driver could see her legs but he would have to angle the mirror downwards if he wanted to see what her hand was doing between them.

'I wanted to touch myself, Patrick, like this . . .' She pulled the thin panel of the panties aside and dipped her finger into her cunt. She ran it up to her clitoris and another moan escaped her lips as

213

she felt it leap, like a startled animal, to her touch. 'They put this long cloak over me and led me into the dining room. They led me round the table, all the men looking at me, wanting me . . .'

She was wanking herself now, circling her clitoris with the tip of her finger, feeling the swollen bud of nerves shooting delicious sensation through her body. She saw Patrick shift uncomfortably in his seat.

'Stop the car, Patrick,' she said quietly.

'No, madam.'

They were nearing the first signs of the suburbs now, leaving the country lanes behind. Soon they would be in a built-up area.

'Oh . . .' Diana gasped involuntarily, as her finger slid against her clitoris.

'No,' the driver said, as if her gasp had been directed at him.

They were on a B-road. About a mile ahead the road widened into a dual carriageway lined by houses. On the left was a field surrounded by a high hedge except for an entrance at one corner, obviously used for tractors. The driver slammed on the brakes of the car. He reversed back up the road to the rutted gap in the hedge, swung the Jaguar through it and stopped under the lee of the hedge. He opened his door as though in a rage, came round to the rear door, flung it open and caught Diana by the hand pulling her bodily from the car.

Without bothering to close either car door he pulled her over to a large oak tree that grew to the side of the track. Under it there was a small patch of grass that had not been churned up by the trac-tor. He literally threw her down on to it, standing over her his face contorted with anger.

'Is this what you want?'

'Yes,' she said, reaching up to the belt of his trousers.

He caught her hand and threw it down.

'No,' he said, unbuckling his belt and pulling his zip down. His trousers fell to his knees. He pulled his pants down. His cock was erect. It was big, uncircumcised and very hairy. She tried to touch it. Again he caught her hand but this time held it tightly by the wrist.

'You want to be fucked, lady?'

'Yes.'

He literally fell on her, fell on her like a hungry wolf. The crotch of her panties was still tucked away in the folds of her thigh. His hands rolled her skirt up to her waist and his big cock lunged into her, right up inside her, so deep she felt it at the neck of her womb, so wide she felt her clitoris stretched taut like an elastic band. He did not move. He made no attempt to pull his cock back. He just pressed it forward, his whole body hard and tight, his muscles locked as he concentrated on boring his cock up into her.

Was it her imagination or did it seem to be going deeper, millimetre by millimetre? She clawed at his arse with her fingers, dug her fingers into his flesh, felt his rigid muscles pushing himself forward.

It was as though her body was melting around him, moulding itself to accommodate this great gourd of flesh. She felt herself opening, blossoming over it, allowing it deeper than any cock had been. He was so rigid, like a huge bone thrust inside her and held there unyielding.

The ground was hard, the grass wet, a stump of exposed root was sticking into her spine, but she felt none of the discomfort. All she could feel was his cock and her body's wanton response.

She started to come. Her body started to churn. She had never felt like this, never had a cock buried so deep, interred in her. She seemed to be able to feel every inch of it, every inch of the hardness and heat. The orgasm that started began in the depths of her cunt, began at the tip of his cock, then joined the waves of sensation from her clitoris, stretched and exposed and crushed against his unmoving pubic bone. It was like an arc of electricity, the current leaping between two points, turning her body into a blue flame and engulfing her. She felt he was fucking her whole body from head to toe. As she came her cunt released a torrent of juices, warm wet juices running down his cock, as though she had spunked.

He felt it too. He pressed forward straining up into her. Her orgasm had allowed him deeper still. His cock began to spasm. It swelled ready to spit out his spunk.

Diana gasped. Her cunt contracted, closing, like a sea anemone around its prey, and clung to his cock. She felt it swell and spasm. It was like being kicked, as it jerked inside her. She could feel his spunk jetting out. It kicked with every gob of spunk. She cried out, with every kick spunk splashing into her body where no spunk had ever been before. She came again, her body trembling, arching, grinding over the tip of his huge cock.

When she opened her eyes it was gloomy and almost dark. Light shone from the open doors of the car, spilling on to the rutted muddy track. It had begun to drizzle and heavy clouds had closed in all round increasing the darkness. The tree had protected them from the rain, its leaves turning brown but still in place.

Patrick got to his feet, pulled his trousers and pants up, zipped up his fly, buckled his belt and got back into the driver's seat. He left the rear door open.

Diana got up. Her coat was covered with grass stains and mud. The back of the black dress was wet where it had lain between her legs. Her panties were soaking wet too, stuck to one side of her thigh. She pulled the crotch back in place but it felt damp and uncomfortable so she tugged them down her legs and put them in her pocket. One of her stockings had been laddered by a twist of bramble extending out of the hedgerow.

Diana got back into the car. As she reached out to close the door she saw her hand was trembling.

Thirty minutes later the Jaguar pulled up outside the main entrance to Harrods. Not a word had been exchanged between them. Nor a look. Diana had watched Patrick's eyes in the rear-view mirror. As far as she could tell he had not looked at her once.

Patrick parked the car at the curb but made no attempt to get out and open the door for her as he had done so assiduously before.

Diana let herself out of the car.

Chapter Nine

'Hi, it's me.' John Borland was 'me'.

'Darling...' Diana said into the phone.

'Are you free tonight?'

'No. I have to go out,' she lied.

'Oh,' he sounded disappointed.

'Sorry, it's business.'

'I'll live. Just.'

'What about Friday?' she suggested.

'Friday's fine. What time?'

'Eight. You can come and pick me up.'

'Can't wait,' he said enthusiastically.

'Me neither.' That was not a lie.

Putting the phone down she sat in an armchair in the living room absent-mindedly watching her husband doing the dusting.

She would have loved to see John Borland tonight but there was a major problem. All the papers had arrived from her solicitors and everything was in order. The survey had shown no faults and the local search revealed nothing untoward so there was no reason not to go ahead with the purchase. Except one. She didn't have the money. She couldn't face John again until she had somehow secured her mortgage. If by Friday she had not managed to see the area manager of the bank then she would have to tell John that he was going to have to start all over again and look for another buyer. It was not a prospect she relished. Until then discretion was very much the better part of valour.

The Royal Palm in Kensington was tucked away in one of the leafy avenues behind the High Street. Diana had arrived on Monday night to be told that Michael Carlton was out and not expected back until after dinner. She had decided not to wait.

On Tuesday Diana arrived at eight o'clock in the evening.

'Mr Carlton, please,' she said to the young man on the reception desk.

He punched the name into his computer terminal. 'Room 354,' he said smiling.

'He's in?'

The man checked the board of keys and corresponding mail slots on the wall behind him.

'He hasn't left his key . . .'

'Thank you.'

Diana could feel his eyes following her as she walked over to the lifts.

On the third floor she followed the arrow on the sign marked ROOMS 351–360 along a corridor carpeted in a rather over-elaborate pattern with a floral wallpaper to match. Outside Room 354 she checked her appearance in the mirror of her compact. She had pinned her hair up and chosen her clothes carefully. Her dress was a dark navy blue with a plunging neckline that revealed acres of her cleavage and a split skirt that uncovered a great deal of thigh.

She decided she needed more lipstick. She applied the flame red colour from the stick in her bag, pouting her lips then sucking on a Kleenex to get rid of the excess.

She knocked twice.

'Coming . . .' she heard a voice shout from inside. She heard a door being closed, the television being switched off. Then the door in front of her opened.

Michael Carlton was in his forties. His face was handsome enough and he had a fine head of hair that had hardly receded at all though its uniform blackness suggested it might have been dyed. He looked as though he had once been a rugby player or footballer in his spare time, but what had once been muscle was now beginning to run to fat. It was easy for Diana to see, as all Michael Carlton was wearing was a small towel knotted around his waist.

'Oh . . .' he said. He had obviously been expecting someone else.

'Room 354,' Diana said. She had rehearsed her entrance.

'Yes?'

'I'm your escort for the evening, Mr Carlton.'

'What?'

'Your escort. You ordered an escort didn't you? Room 354?'

'How did you know my name?'

'They gave it to me. Is anything wrong?'

'Yes. I mean no. I mean . . . You'd better come in . . .' Carlton scanned the corridor checking to see if anyone else had seen her. There was no one else about.

221

Diana walked into the bedroom. It was the usual modern hotel bedroom, cramped for space and decorated with total anonymity. It had the usual furniture; a thinly mattressed double bed, bedside tables attached to the headboard, a trouser press screwed to the wall, two bucket shaped armchairs and a small television perched on a one-drawed table opposite the bed. The tiny bathroom just managed to contain a bath and a toilet.

'Look, I think there's been a mistake,' Carlton said, pulling on a towelling robe. Unfortunately as he did the little towel fell off and Diana glimpsed his thick dark pubic hair and the flaccid tube of his cock, before he hurriedly tied the robe.

'Eight-fifteen. Room 354 . . .' Diana said. She stripped off her coat and sat down on the bed, crossing her legs so the split skirt would reveal the welt of her sheer flesh-coloured stocking.

'No, but you're the wrong girl.'

That was a response Diana had not anticipated. 'The wrong girl . . .' she said.

'It's always the same girl. I always have the same girl. Every month. She's not ill, is she? They didn't say anything on the phone about her being ill. Why didn't they tell me?'

'Oh . . .' Diana was trying to think of something to say. Her plan was to pretend he had ordered an escort, get into his room and use her obvious charms to seduce him. It seemed Mr Carlton had already ordered an escort. And Diana could think of nothing else to do but make her apologies and leave.

'There must have been a mistake . . . I think . . .'

The loud rap on the door interrupted her.

'Oh . . .' Carlton looked confused.

'I'd better go,' Diana said, standing up. She reached for her coat.

The rap on the bedroom door was louder this time. Carlton looked, for some reason Diana could not understand, like a scared rabbit.

'I've got to answer . . .' he said, realising there was no way of getting Diana out of the room before he opened the door.

'Don't worry, I'll explain,' Diana said glumly. Her attempt to suborn the area manager was going to end in failure.

He opened the door.

'What the hell you keeping me waiting for, you white honky bastard. You're going to pay for this.'

Dressed in a black leather coat and leather boots and carrying the sort of bag doctors use, the black woman pushed past Carlton and marched into the room. Diana recognised her at once.

'Domina!' she exclaimed.

'Kirsty! What the hell are you doing here?'

'There's been a mix-up . . .'

'With this idiot it doesn't surprise me.' Domina said. Turning to Carlton she snapped, 'Close that damn door and get that robe off. What's the matter with you?'

'I'll go . . .' Diana said.

'Why don't you stay? This little worm can afford it. Can't you, honky. You want a special treat with Mistress Kirsty?'

Carlton looked bemused. 'Yes, Mistress.'

'You're a very lucky honky. Mistress Kirsty is my friend. My good friend. She can help me deal with you. Aren't you lucky?'

223

Carlton took money from the inside of a paper-back book lying on the table near the television. He searched for his wallet in his jacket that hung in the small open wardrobe by the door. He handed Domina a stack of notes. Domina counted out five fifties and handed them to Diana. She turned so Carlton couldn't see her face and winked.

'Now get your robe off and assume the position.'

Carlton pulled the robe off and knelt on the floor immediately. He pressed his forehead into the carpet, his arse in the air.

'So, how have you been? Domina asked, as casually as if they had met in the supermarket.

'Fine. You?' Diana said, trying not to let her unease into her voice.

'Great. Haven't seen you since the party. Some party eh?' Great spread. God, I got pissed.'

Domina stripped off the black leather coat. Her skin was black, a very dark black, with her hair cropped to no more than an inch in length and matted in tight curls. Under the coat she wore a leather halter top decorated with six or seven layers of chains strung across her bosom one on top of the other. Below the halter was a band of naked flesh separating it from the miniscule black leather skirt she wore. Her legs were clad in fishnet stockings, their tops and the leather suspenders that held them in place, both well below the hem of the skirt.

Domina was pear-shaped. The halter top hid little in the way of tits, but from her waist down her figure flared out into a big meaty arse and plump fleshy thighs.

'I thought you worked from your own place?'

Diana said, remembering the room where she had
first encountered Domina with her husband
Charles strapped down to a punishment frame.

'Not always. Sometimes I come calling.' She
opened the leather bag and extracted a tangle of
leather straps dropping them on the bed, their
buckles tinkling like tiny bells. They looked like
a writhing mass of black snakes. She pulled out a
riding crop that had been doubled over in the bag
and a thick rectangular of leather about two feet
long and three inches wide with a cut-out at one
end to form a handle. Without a word, Domina
raised the crop and stroked it down on Carlton's
backside. He moaned. Domina gave him five sharp
blows then sat down on the bed. His head had not
moved from the carpet.

Domina nodded encouragement at Diana.

'Lick my feet,' Diana said, unzipping her dress.
Carlton inched forward on his knees. Diana pulled
the dress over her head to reveal the black basque
she had so carefully chosen. This basque was not
rigid and boned like the more common type but
stretchy and elastic, woven with Lycra so it seemed
to shine. It was light and clinging and transparent,
its suspenders were not hooked into little loops at
the hem but part of the design, loops of material
forming long fingers over her thighs. She had not
bothered to wear panties.

Carlton had not begun his work.

'Do as she tells you, honky,' Domina ordered,
reinforcing the message with a slash of the whip.

Carlton started licking immediately. He licked
the black leather of the court shoes and the tops
of her nylon covered feet. Diana remembered her

husband doing the same thing at Domina's bidding.

'That's enough,' Diana said, using the same tone she had come to adopt with her husband. She smiled to herself. She had suddenly realised that her attempt to seduce Michael Carlton was not going to be a failure after all. It fact it was going to succeed better than she could have imagined.

'Stand up,' Domina ordered. Carlton obeyed, standing in the middle of the room his eyes cast down to his feet, his hands clasped firmly behind his back and his cock poking out in front of him fully erect. His bottom was already red from the attention of Domina's whip.

Untangling a strap from the pile on the bed Domina used it to bind his wrists behind his back.

'Down,' she barked.

It was a well-rehearsed ritual. Carlton positioned himself in the middle of the bed face down.

'Would you like to have a piece of this worm, Kirsty?' Domina knelt on the bed besides him.

'Why not?'

'Here,' Domina handed her the leather paddle. 'Use this. How many shall Mistress Kirsty give you, worm?' How many do you deserve?'

'I've been good, Mistress,' Carlton said pathetically.

'It's for me to tell you whether you've been good or not isn't it?'

'Yes, Mistress.'

Diana practised with the paddle, swishing it through the air to gauge its weight.

'We'll start with six,' Domina said, pulling his bound hands up into the small of his back.

Diana knelt on the bed opposite Domina, Carlton's white unmuscled buttocks laid out between them. She raised the paddle to shoulder level.

'Count,' Domina ordered.

The leather whistled through the air and landed with a resounding thwack.

'One,' he breathed through gritted teeth.

'Harder,' Domina mouthed at Diana without pronouncing the word.

Diana raised her arm higher and put more effort into her drive. The paddle swung through the air and Carlton's body convulsed as the smack of leather on flesh echoed through the room.

'Two.'

Diana was reminded of her husband, intoning the numbers as Domina had trained him to do. As she slashed the next four strokes down in quick succession and Carlton wriggled under the blows she thought the beating would end in the same result.

It did not.

'Right,' Domina said. She got up from the bed. The pile of belts and harnesses had fallen to the floor. She put them back on the bed and extracted two long thick belts which she quickly strapped around his ankles and just above his knees. Going to the doctor's bag she pulled out a leather hood. She drew it over Carlton's head and secured it in place by means for a draw-string at its base. Almost as an afterthought, she freed another strap from the tangle and cinched it around his elbows in exactly the same way as Diana had been tied by the housekeeper.

The hood had no holes for his eyes or mouth. It

had a small opening for his nostrils.

'Right,' she said, picking up her leather coat and putting it back on, 'drinky-poohs . . .'

'What?'

'Put your dress on. We're going downstairs for a drink. You can leave your coat here.'

Diana slipped back into the dress. Domina took the room key, turned the lights off, hung the 'Do Not Disturb' notice on the door handle and locked the door behind them.

'Now we go down to the bar for half an hour.' Domina explained.

'Why?'

'He likes to be left like that . . . A lot of them do.' They took the lift down to the bar chatting inconsequentially about Carolyn's party. It was not until they were sitting in the rather austere bar of the hotel, its walls covered with fake wooden beams and horse brasses in an attempt to make it look like a country pub, that Domina raised the subject of what in the world 'Kirsty' was doing there.

Diana decided there was no point in lying. As she told Domina the real reason for her presence in Carlton's room the black woman starting laughing, a deep husky laugh.

'Well, you certainly get A for effort . . .'

'I had no idea he was into all this. Is he a regular?'

'Regular as clockwork. Once a month. Never fails. Won't come to me though. I always have to travel. Think he's afraid I might have two-way mirrors and cameras or something. Anyway, like most of them, it's a set routine. Beat his big white arse. Tie him up. Leave him. Down here for a drink. A

228

little play-acting when I go back. Turn him over and a couple of quick wanks and he comes like gang busters . . .'

There were two rather elderly men sitting on the other side of the bar. Diana saw one of them turn his head at the word 'wank'. He eyed both women speculatively and said something to his friend who also looked round.

'He told me he likes to imagine some strange woman wandering into the wrong room . . .' Domina caught the waiter's eye. They were drinking champagne. She ordered another glass, charging it to Carlton's room. 'Incidentally that guy you helped me out with a few weeks back. Haven't seen him since. He used to be one of my regulars.'

The 'guy' was Diana's husband. She had given no clue to Domina at the time of his identity.

'Really?' she said.

'Yeah. You haven't seen him? He used to be a good customer.'

'Me, no.' Diana said quietly. She smiled to herself. Now she knew Charles hadn't sneaked off for a private visit with Domina. He was obviously getting all he could take at home.

They finished their champagne and wandered back through the ground-floor lobby looking at the display panels where West End jewellers, leather goods manufacturers, and clothes shops had samples of their wares on view to tempt tourists to look up their premises. It was almost exactly half an hour later when Domina let them back into Carlton's bedroom.

'Come in, darling . . .' Domina said loudly putting on the lights and taking off her coat. She put the back of her hand to her mouth and kissed it making a deliberately exaggerated lip-smacking sound. 'Let's give him his money's worth,' she whispered to Diana.

Diana was quick on the up-take. 'Oh, I don't think I should.'

'Come here. Let me teach you the ways of love.' She made another kissing sound with her hand, longer and more pronounced.

'I've never done it before with a woman.'

'Oh Jesus, what's this? We must have got into the wrong room. Look honey . . .'

'He's all tied up.'

'Well, let's have a look at him . . .'

Domina knelt on the bed and rolled Carlton over. His erection sprung up vertically. It was red and angry looking, every vein, every blood vessel straining for release.

'Well, he's a big boy,' Domina said.

'Pity to waste it,' Diana added kneeling opposite Domina again. 'You take the balls, I'll take the cock.'

'He's making me feel really hot.'

Diana cupped Carlton's balls. They were big and hairy and felt incredibly hot. Domina circled the rim of his glans with her hand then stopped.

'I don't know. We shouldn't do this.'

Carlton's body strained off the bed. The hood didn't gag him but he said nothing.

'Oh, let's,' Diana said, squeezing his balls. A tear of fluid had formed on the top of his cock.

Domina wanked down with her hand. By the time the ring she had made with her thumb and forefinger had come up again Diana could feel his balls pulsing and see his cock twitching. In an instant spunk lashed out into the air. A speck splashed on Domina's leather halter, most landed on Carlton's navel. He moaned loudly and bucked his hips as though trying to fuck Domina's hand. As the tension in his body eased, more spunk seeped from his cock and over Domina's fingers.

Domina got to her feet and went into the bathroom to wash the spunk from her hand. 'You can untie him,' she shouted.

Diana started unbuckling the straps that held him. Domina came back and unfastened the drawstring of the hood. She pulled it off his head. His face was swathed in sweat, his hair standing on end.

Stuffing all the equipment back into the doctor's bag, Domina put her leather coat on again. Diana picked up her coat but did not bother to put it on.

'Thanks for your help, makes a change for him.' Domina winked.

Carlton did not say a word. He had pulled a sheet up over his body and turned on his side, his eyes closed.

'Always the same,' Domina whispered, 'sleeps like a baby.'

They let themselves out of the bedroom turning the lights out as they went. Domina did not notice that Diana had slipped the room key into her bag.

'See you again some time, honey,' Domina said kissing her on the cheek as she hailed a taxi outside the hotel. She climbed aboard and it pulled away.

Diana took a taxi too. She asked to be taken to

231

the nearest all-night chemist.

A noise woke him. He couldn't see his watch on the bedside table so he didn't know what time it was. He couldn't tell what the noise had been. Hotels were full of strange noises he told himself. Then he realised it had been the noise of his bedroom door closing. He heard the unmistakable sound of the long zip of a dress singing as it parted and the rustle as the dress was discarded. Another rustle as lingerie was pulled off. He felt the bed give next to him and the warmth and softness of a female body snuggling up next to him.

'Oh, darling,' the woman said, 'You know what I'd like to do?'

'No . . .' he murmured so she wouldn't recognise his voice.

The body pressed into him. He felt her soft thighs wrapping around him. He could feel big fleshy tits.

'Let's play our game, darling. I feel so sexy.'

A hand was pulling a sleeping mask over his eyes. He should have torn it off and reached for the light switch but he didn't. He should have told this woman she was making a mistake, that she was in the wrong room, but he didn't. His cock was rock hard . . .

It had happened when he was thirteen. His parents had taken him to a seaside hotel, the first time he'd ever been to a hotel. He'd woken in the middle of the night to find a woman climbing into bed next to him. She'd smelt of whisky. She was in the wrong room. She was drunk. She rolled in to him and screamed. She said it was his fault, he was in the wrong bed. She'd pulled him over her knee and spanked him, told him how bad he was. She felt his cock. It was hard. She told him that was bad too. But instead of spanking him for that too she pulled off her nightdress and wound it over his head so he wouldn't see. She'd taken his penis, held him down. He could smell her body on the nightdress. He could feel the lips of her sex, hairy and hot . . .

What was this woman doing now? It felt like a bandage. She was tying his arms up with a bandage, tying them tight behind his back. This was real. This was actually happening. This was not the performance he paid so much money for every month. This was a real mistake.

She tied his legs too, winding the bandage around them tightly so he couldn't move. He should tell her she was making a mistake.

'Darling . . .' she said, her voice deep with passion, 'now you can't resist me. Now I can do whatever I want with you . . .'

She turned him on his back. Surely now, he thought, she would realise her mistake.

Her mouth engulfed his cock. He felt her hands on his balls. He hadn't felt as excited as this since, since . . .

The woman's mouth felt hot. Incredibly hot. He knew he was going to spunk. He knew there was nothing he could do to stop it. Her mouth gobbled him up. She mumbled the words, his cock still in her mouth. But he knew what they meant.

'Give it to me,' she'd said.

And he did.

Chapter Ten

It was even quicker than Diana expected. On Thursday morning as Diana was getting ready for her aerobics class the phone rang.

'Mrs Wilson? It's Appleby at the bank.'

'Hello, Mr Appleby.'

'I thought you'd like to know right away. Your mortgage application has been approved.'

Diana was not surprised.

'Apparently the area manager, Mr Carlton, had no objections.'

'I didn't think he would.'

'You managed to get to see him then?'

'I refuse to answer on the grounds that I might incriminate myself . . .'

Appleby laughed. 'You can be very persuasive.'

'Yes, I suppose I can.'

'Well, we'll send everything to your solicitors.'

'Thank you for letting me know.'

'Any time, Ms Wilson.' He said, the double meaning quite intentional judging by the tone of voice.

Diana grinned broadly as she put the phone down. Michael Carlton had been as good as his word. He had assured her that 'her little problem', as he'd called it, would be solved with no difficulty.

In fact, he had told her, she should feel free to come to him for whatever she wanted. She had made him, however temporarily, a very happy man.

Now Diana could make plans, and face John Borland with a clear conscience. She could also see to it that his remaining weeks in England, before he slipped off to Texas, were full and satisfying.

She realised she would miss him when he was gone. Perhaps in other circumstances she might even have fallen in love with him. He was strong and powerful physically, and witty and charming intellectually as well as being extremely attractive. But at the moment she could not imagine wanting to be tied to any one man however alluring. She might want the adventure she had embarked on to end one day but at the moment, that day was a long way in the future.

John Borland was a source of delight but, as she remembered a Swedish friend once telling her, why settle for one dish when you can have smorgasbord?

Tomorrow night however, was a prospect she relished, particularly now it would not have to include any unpleasant truths. She had not been looking forward to telling John she couldn't buy his house after all. Now that shadow had disappeared she could concentrate on matters much closer to her heart.

The telephone rang again just as she was going out of the front door.

'Kirsty. It's Carolyn.'

'Oh, hi. You just caught me. I was walking out of the front door.'

'I was ringing to find out if you were free tonight. I've got a job for you . . .'

'Tonight's fine . . .'

'Good. Eight o'clock. The Park View Hotel. In the bar. Mr MacIntosh. He'll recognise you.'

'How?'

'Oh, I . . . I . . . showed him your picture.'

'All right, I'll be there.' In all her dealings with Carolyn's Escorts, Carolyn had never called her personally. 'Is Maggie ill or something?' Diana asked.

'No, no. She's here. She's busy at the moment that's all.' Carolyn's voice sounded strained.

'Say hello for me, then,' Diana said. They exchanged goodbyes.

As Diana locked her front door she puzzled over the telephone conversation. There was something in the tone of Carolyn's voice that she did not understand. Perhaps Mr MacIntosh was an old friend, someone she wanted to deal with personally, but if that was the case why hadn't she said so. It was very odd.

Diana sat on the barstool at the bar of the Park View Hotel. Mr MacIntosh was late. Twenty minutes late. Diana had nursed her Perrier until all its ice had melted.

'Kirsty?' A man tapped her on the shoulder. She had not noticed him approach.

'Yes.' Diana wheeled round on the stool to face him.

'MacIntosh,' he said.

'Hi there.'

'Sorry, I'm so late. Would you mind if I had a drink first? I really need a drink.' His voice sounded gruff and tense.

'No, of course not.'

MacIntosh ordered a large gin and tonic and sat on the bar stool beside her. He was not a big man, thin, almost painfully thin, with a soft face and rather long hair that had been groomed with hair-cream making it look darker than it actually was.

Diana stared at his face. For some reason he appeared familiar.

MacIntosh consumed the gin like a man who had spent the day in a desert.

'Right,' he said. He helped Diana down from the bar stool. She was wearing a modest grey shirt-waister. It was not a good idea to wear anything too obvious in West End hotels. Hotel security was strict. 'Nice legs,' he added.

'Why, thank you.'

In the lift MacIntosh handed Diana five fifty-pound notes without a word. Diana put them in her bag. He appeared not to want to indulge in small talk. They stood in the lift in silence. He looked straight ahead not looking at her.

His room was small. The usual hotel furniture but, to match the pretensions of the establishment, it had been styled to look antique. There was no sign of any of MacIntosh's things, no cases, no clothes. He had obviously hired the room for the sole purpose of using it for their liaison.

MacIntosh picked up her hand and kissed it deli-cately. His hands felt soft. His nails were mani-cured. Diana felt a little thrill of excitement at his touch. He looked into her eyes for one half of one second, then looked away quickly.

'Would you get into bed . . .' he said.

'Don't you want to watch me undress?'

'No.'

'I'm wearing stockings . . . shall I keep them on?'

'No. Excuse me.' He turned abruptly and went into the bathroom shutting the door firmly behind him and locking it.

Diana unbuttoned her dress and hung it over the back of one of the small armchairs in the room. There was barely room to move around the double bed. She had made up for the plainness of her outer layers by wearing her sexiest lingerie. Apparently her efforts had been wasted. MacIntosh was not interested in watching her peel away the deep cut underwired bra fashioned in sea-blue silk and satin, nor the matching French knickers split at both sides almost to the waist, nor the wide satin suspender belt that covered half her navel and held up her sheer grey stockings.

Naked, Diana climbed between the sheets. The maid had already turned down the bed. She heard the bathroom door open, but he remained where she could not see him.

'I'd like the lights out, please,' he said.

She found a switch to the side of the headboard and the room was plunged into darkness. MacIntosh picked his way over to the bed. He sat on the edge of it and for a moment did nothing. Diana had the feeling he was deciding whether he should go on.

'Don't be nervous,' she said trying to reassure him. She put a hand out to touch his shoulder and discovered he was wearing a T-shirt.

'I am nervous,' he said, the gruffness of his voice giving way to an altogether lighter tone.

Suddenly he pulled himself up on to the bed, found Diana, wrapped his arm around her shoulders and kissed her full on the mouth. At the same time his other hand was groping for her breasts, seizing one at a time, pinching her nipples, kneading the heavy flesh, like a man who had been deprived of contact for a very long time. He broke the kiss and started kissing her throat instead. His hand left her breasts and slid over her navel. His mouth replaced it, licking and sucking at each of her nipples in turn. His fingers found the V of her thighs and pushed down into her hairy labia almost before she'd had time to open her legs. There was no subtlety, no finesse. Diana sensed a strange desperation which she did not understand.

Diana felt him working his cock against her thigh rhythmically, but his cock was still only semi-erect. She wanted to tell him to slow down, to take it more gently, but decided that would only make him more nervous. She tried to move, to take his cock in her hand, but he twisted away.

'No,' he said.

'Let me suck it,' she said. 'I love that.'

'No, no, no . . .'

He mounted her. She opened her legs wider and he immediately pushed what there was of his erection against her labia. His foreplay – or was it the situation? – had made her wet. He was using his hand to cram his cock into her sex. She felt it penetrate but only a very little. He started fucking her with it nevertheless, desperately, much too desperately, trying to make it bigger. She did what she could to help. She wrapped her arms around his back and hugged him to her. She found his ear and stuck her tongue into it as deep as it would go. But his cock got no bigger.

He rolled off her. The slight erection he had achieved disappeared entirely. He curled into a foetal position his back turned away from her.

'Don't worry,' she said. 'It can happen to anyone.'

'Put the light on.' This voice was quite different. It was a voice she recognised. Diana flipped the light switch.

'I'm sorry, Kirsty...' Carolyn said, turning over to face Diana. No wonder the face had been so familiar.

'Carolyn?'

'I'm really sorry. I thought... I just wanted... It's difficult to explain.'

'Why didn't you tell me?'

'It was a crazy idea. I just wanted to see if I could be a man again. I found you so attractive. You did such wonderful things to me. I thought if I could be a man with anyone it would be you...'

'Oh, Carolyn. I should be flattered...'

'It was a stupid idea. I knew it wasn't going to work as soon as we walked into the bedroom. I've been taking the hormones for too long. At least I can stop putting on that silly voice.'

Carolyn started to get out of the bed.

'Where are you going?'

'There's no point prolonging this charade.'

'And what about me?'

'What do you mean?'

'You've got me all worked up. The least you can do is finish what you started.' Carolyn looked into Diana's eyes. Her expression was determined, she was not going to take no for an answer. 'And take that T-shirt off, I want to see your breasts.'

'I thought...' Carolyn stuttered.

'You thought what? That I was drunk last time? That you took advantage of me? Well I wasn't and you didn't. I wanted you as a woman. I think of you as a woman. I find you very attractive. I want you as a woman now.'

Carolyn felt a surge of excitement. She knew Diana was telling the truth. She could see it in her eyes. She pulled the T-shirt over her head. Immediately, Diana leant forward and took her nascent breasts in her hand. She pulled Carolyn back down on to the bed, pinching her nipples with her fingernails, then taking them one by one into her mouth. She sucked them hungrily, taking the whole breast between her lips then using her teeth on the nipple. Carolyn gasped.

'Finish what you started, Carolyn . . .' Diana said, her voice deep with passion.

She lay back on the bed, her legs open, both bent at the knee. Carolyn came up on to her knees. She kissed Diana on the mouth as she had done before, then licked down her long sinewy neck to her breasts. She paused there, licking and sucking and nibbling, then moved her mouth down to her navel while her hand ran up Diana's thigh and into her thick labia. Her tongue descended into the cleft of her sex, teasing the clitoris out from its fleshy confinement as her finger probed into the wetness of Diana's cunt. It was Diana's turn to gasp.

Carolyn reached out with her other hand to gather Diana's breast. She knelt between her open legs. With her lips she sucked the whole of Diana's labia into her mouth, then found the clitoris again and tapped it with her tongue as she put one, then two, then three fingers inside the warm wet cunt, crammed them in and pushed them as deep as they would go.

She used her fingers like a cock, thrusting them in and out while her tongue flicked Diana's clitoris from side to side.

It brought Diana off. She felt her body tense, preparing itself for the onslaught of feeling that this strange woman – a woman with a cock that was how Diana thought of her – was wringing out of her body. She raised her hips off the bed allowing Carolyn's mouth more freedom on her sex, allowing her fingers to go deeper.

'Oh, Carolyn . . .' she gasped. And then the feelings took over and a warmth and blackness flooded her body, and she felt every muscle in her body lock up, like the links in a chain suddenly pulled tight. And just as suddenly the tension snapped, the chain broken, her body released to wallow in incredible sensation.

When she finally opened her eyes again, Carolyn was looking down at her with an expression of pure pleasure.

'Thank you,' Carolyn said.

'For what?'

'For not laughing at my stupidity.'

'Will you do something for me, Carolyn?'

'Anything.'

'Put my stockings on, my knickers, everything. And make-up. There's some in my bag.'

Carolyn looked puzzled. 'Why?'

'Just do it, will you?'

'If that's what you want.'

'It is.'

Diana got up and looked in the minibar the room

243

was equipped with. There was a half bottle of
champagne inside. She opened it and poured it into
two glasses while Carolyn sat using her make-up,
expertly applying mascara, eye shadow and lipstick. The shades were much brighter than she
normally wore, but that didn't matter. As soon as
she stared at herself in the mirror, her face high-
lighted by the make-up, her cheekbones accentu-
ated, her green eyes emphasised, her lips pouting
in lipstick, she felt better. She combed her hair
back, getting rid of the parting, combing it
straight back. Despite the haircream it looked feminine enough.

'That's better,' Diana declared. 'For God's sake,
Carolyn that's how you belong. You're beautiful.'

Carolyn clipped the blue suspender belt around
her waist and sat on the bed rolling on the stockings. Her legs were long, smooth and hairless. She
pulled the French knickers up over her hips, enjoying the feeling of the soft silk against her flesh.

'Does that feel good?' Diana asked.

'Very. I don't think the bra will fit.'

'Now come and lie here.'

Diana took a sip of champagne and Carolyn did
the same. Then she lay back on the bed. Diana lay
beside her, pressing her big breasts into Carolyn's
side. Her hand roamed the silk knickers, the grey
stockings, the suspender belt.

'This is how you should be,' she whispered as she
rolled on top of her.

She moved her flat navel against Carolyn, slowly
at first, then with more purpose. She ran her hands
over Carolyn's legs again, feeling the creamy flesh
above the stocking-tops.

'You're a real woman, Carolyn. So feminine. So soft.'

She could feel Carolyn's penis between their bodies. It was only half-erect but Carolyn was moaning, tossing her head from side to side, her hands stretched out above her head.

'Oh, Kirsty . . .'

'Yes, feel like a woman. Feel it.'

Diana's rhythm increased as though she was fucking Carolyn, her iron-flat belly riding over the little penis, covered in silky knickers.

'Come for me . . .' she whispered, as she moved relentlessly, her naked body moulding itself to Carolyn, her big breasts pressed against Carolyn's tiny bosom.

'I want it, darling . . .'

She felt Carolyn tense. She felt her body pulled taut by her nerves. Her head stopped rolling. She made a noise, a strange almost animal noise, like a sob of pain mixed with a cry of ecstasy. She brought her arms down to her thighs and stroked the silk of the knickers and nylon of the stockings as if reassuring herself that they were real. Then she sighed, a long contented sigh and Diana felt a patch of wetness spreading through the knickers and over her navel.

'You're wonderful, Diana, do you know that?' Carolyn said, when all the little tremors and sensations of the aftermath had finally abated. 'I think it's a talent. You just seem to know exactly the right thing to say. And do. No wonder you're so popular.'

'I feel it too,' Diana said truthfully. It was like a sixth sense, she thought, reaching into the sexual

psyche to pluck out what had been ignored, suppressed, worried over. It was a talent. And like any
talent, Diana got enormous pleasure from exercis-
ing it. It was her life now after all. Not a life
imposed on her by social conventions, by what
people expected her to do and be. But the life she
had chosen, and the life she wanted.

The front door was ajar when John Borland arrived
ten minutes after eight on Friday night. He opened
it cautiously and closed it behind him.

In the hall a dress lay discarded. A little further
on lay a black high-heeled shoe. At the foot of the
stairs there was a black stocking. He picked it up.
The sheer nylon gave him a frisson of pleasure
as he remembered how it had looked on Diana's
long legs.

He climbed the stairs. Half way up was the
second high-heeled shoe. On the top step was a
black lacy bra, its big cups leaving no doubt as to
its owner. John picked that up too and held the
lacy material to his face. It smelt of Diana's
perfume.

A little way down the landing lay a black suspender belt. It was still attached to one black stocking. In front of the bedroom door there was a pair
of tiny lacy black panties. John picked the knickers
up too. They felt warm as if they had only just
been taken off ...

He opened the bedroom door slowly. On the floor
inside, to his surprise, was another shoe, in a bigger
size, and a few inches away another stocking. He
couldn't see any further into the room as it was
dark. He groped for the light switch but before he

could find it the bedside lamp was switched on . . .

'Surprise!' two voices said in unison.

Lying naked in each other's arms on the bed, Diana and Ann grinned broadly. A trail of Ann's clothing led across the carpet to the foot of the bed.

'Come in, the water's fine,' Ann said.

'I'm afraid we started without you,' Diana told him, licking her lips and tasting again the slight saltiness of her friend's sex.

Headline Delta Erotic Survey

In order to provide the kind of books you like to read - and to qualify for a free erotic novel of the Editor's choice - we would appreciate it if you would complete the following survey and send your answers, together with any further comments, to:

Headline Book Publishing
FREEPOST (WD 4984)
London
NW1 0YR

1. Are you male or female?
2. Age? Under 20 / 20 to 30 / 30 to 40 / 40 to 50 / 50 to 60 / 60 to 70 / over
3. At what age did you leave full-time education?
4. Where do you live? (Main geographical area)
5. Are you a regular erotic book buyer / a regular book buyer in general / both?
6. How much approximately do you spend a year on erotic books / on books in general?
7. How did you come by this book?
7a. If you bought it, did you purchase from:
   a national bookchain / a high street store / a newsagent / a motorway station / an airport / a railway station / other........
8. Do you find erotic books easy / hard to come by?
8a. Do you find Headline Delta erotic books easy / hard to come by?
9. Which are the best / worst erotic books you have ever read?
9a. Which are the best / worst Headline Delta erotic books you have ever read?
10. Within the erotic genre there are many periods, subjects and literary styles. Which of the following do you prefer:
10a. (period) historical / Victorian / C20th / contemporary / future?
10b. (subject) nuns / whores & whorehouses / Continental frolics / s&m / vampires / modern realism / escapist fantasy / science fiction?

10c. (styles) hardboiled / humorous / hardcore / ironic / romantic / realistic?

10d. Are there any other ingredients that particularly appeal to you?

11. We try to create a cover appearance that is suitable for each title. Do you consider them to be successful?

12. Would you prefer them to be less explicit / more explicit?

13. We would be interested to hear of your other reading habits. What other types of books do you read?

14. Who are your favourite authors?

15. Which newspapers do you read?

16. Which magazines?

17. Do you have any other comments or suggestions to make?

If you would like to receive a free erotic novel of the Editor's choice (available only to UK residents), together with an up-to-date listing of Headline Delta titles, please supply your name and address. Please allow 28 days for delivery.

Name..

Address..

....

....

A selection of Erotica
from Headline